Women
of the
Round Table

Phibby Venable

Women of the Round Table

Copyright © 2010 by Phibby Venable

ISBN: 978-0-9846216-7-5

Library of Congress Control Number: 2010913596

Cover Design by All Things That Matter Press

Published in 2010 by All Things That Matter Press

This book is dedicated to my family & friends.
A special thank you to Ralph Ramsden, a steady
support in a chaotic life & to Deb, for her endless editing,
kindness and patience with a first time novelist.
Also great appreciation to Jean, Judy, Jan, Gidget,
Kristie, Jill, Jeannie, Ashley Jane, and Paula.
A hug to Brook for her wonderful suggestions &
to Autumn for her loyal assistance in the face of more
fun things to do...

Chapter One

Katie leaned in the door, a daffodil in her puffy yellow fluff jacket, her yellow hair swinging. We were all in our forties, with the exception of Alba, but Katie appeared much younger. The wheels of time had taken a detour around her soft skin and vibrant eyes, not to mention her still-youthful heart.

She was the first to arrive for Friday night coffee. Katie loved parties as much as she hated rules. She had a reputation for personality, charm, and certain abilities when it came to the husbands of other women to perform with vivacious agility. It wasn't that she chose married men, more that the married men failed to mention partners and implied in every way that they were single.

Everyone came easily to her command: mechanics, plumbers, police officers, the local motorcycle gang. Katie had no prejudices. She usually had a full house when she sang on Monday nights at the karaoke bar. She's my baby sister's best friend. Katie and Kat, Kat and Katie, where there's one, the other is not far behind.

Anyway, each Friday night we meet for coffee – cream and sugar, solid black, it doesn't matter – we like to gather to chat. So many things were changing, and we needed to hold tight to our closeness. We chose to do that through discussion, sharing a general overview of our lives, each person throwing out a lot or a bit, each person pulling in for a time, sharing tales of anti-social and tiresome despair, of joy, or, most often and most fatal, tales of love.

I saw Kat pull into the driveway and raise a middle finger toward the street. Kat had little patience; she was famous her road rage, at odds with her willingness to give anyone a chance, but also a swift insult. And Kat could really yell. She had a gift for looking vicious, but possessed a golden heart that interfered with her facade. It was always difficult for her to decide between sweet and swear.

I saw my neighbor, Alba, cutting through the yard. She was a Friday night staple who would never miss the opportunity to listen while Kat and Katie discussed the sexual positions of their latest lusts. A neat woman in her pale, matching suit, Alba's hair was always perfectly coiffed, her inevitable pointed-toed shoes sharp and well-heeled.

Everything about her came off as pure, ladylike, and dependable. She appeared to be somewhere in her sixties, but no one knew for sure. It always seemed too rude to ask.

Alba was insecure in a lot of ways, but, oh, her cooking! Indescribable. And, sure enough, she carried with her a round plastic-lidded dish, alone enough to secure her entry. The best cook in town was always welcome at our gatherings.

It looked like a foursome for the evening. We'd sometimes had a fifth, Darrie Demar, but she was in jail for a little event that involved a money order her boyfriend sent. It turned out to be illegal and the police caught his "ring", which consisted of him and Darrie, who had no idea that people stole money orders 'til she was behind bars.

Kat was carrying banana bread and a new flavored creamer. She wasn't one to be outdone by anyone. She liked Alba, but was a great cook in her own right and had no intention of giving in graciously to what she considered Alba's attempt to dominate the snacks. I wasn't too thrilled with the creamer. I never am, but Kat persists. I like coffee that tastes just like coffee. Nothing sweet. I go to hot chocolate for that. Still, I love persistence in anyone. It's a great character trait.

Kat raged into the house complaining, "Did you see that idiot? If he had followed any closer, he would have been up my rear instead of on it."

"What did he look like?" Katie asked hopefully, the word rear attracting her attention.

"Oh, and did I mention," Kat was ignoring the interruption, "that the left lane is for passing? Passing me would have been too simple, though, too much common sense involved."

"I think I recognize that car," Alba chimed in. "I think he has circled this house before." Her love for drama was too well known, so no one went for the bait she dangled.

I poured coffee for everyone and we sat down at the round table. It was a huge table that I had found at a flea market and simply had to have. The chairs were long since broken so now it was circled by an assortment of no-two-alike replacements. It was sleek, hard wood, darker in spots from human sweat and steaming plates. The table had a great attitude and never gave an inch or skid when a person grew too violent or jocular or ill bred.

Everyone settled comfortably in a sit or a sprawl. Just then the doorbell rang.

"Who else is coming?" Katie was leaning toward the window to try to catch a glimpse.

"No one else," I said, heading for the door. I opened it to an empty street and an equally empty stoop. Probably some kid acting the fool. I almost had the door shut when I noticed a splash of yellow at the edge of the door. I leaned over to study it more. It looked like a large ball covered with wrapping tissue. I grabbed it and took it inside, curious. It seemed to glow in my hands, as though I held the moon. I carried it in and placed it on the table.

"Does this belong to anyone?"

"Perhaps it fell off Kat's banana bread," Alba said.

Katie leaned closer. "What crappy wrapping," she said. "I hate it when people wrap things in tissue. It's like handing over a present in its underwear."

"Perhaps Alba planned to light it later and have us all stomp," Kat said. Alba was instantly offended, but I laughed. It made an amusing picture.

"Just open it," Katie said.

We studied the yellow blob in the middle of the table for at least five seconds and then opened it. In the middle of winter even a bomb would be okay, something to shake up the boredom. It was not a bomb, but an impressive set of microphones and karaoke music. Katie and Kat both squealed with delight.

"Somebody loves me!" Katie said smugly. Kat was instantly offended.

"What makes you think it's for you," she said, but Katie was smiling with the assurance of a well-fed cat.

"Anyone else here wearing yellow," she asked. "Anyone else here have a stalker circling the block?" Everyone leaned back in acceptance. It made perfect sense, the car circling, the yellow to match Katie's hair, and, most obvious of all, the stalking. No one here had stalkers but Katie. It was a known fact that at least three men in town knew where Katie was at any given moment.

"Well," Kat said, "at least there are two of them, as in one for me and one for you." Katie grinned and nodded agreeably. We spent the rest of the evening commenting on the music, the food, and stalkers in general. Then Katie heard Montel on the TV in the den, Sylvia Brown pushing blender buttons. Katie has a passion for Montel and Sylvia so she stayed in the den to watch for a second, then gathered her yellow wrappings and headed home to watch it on her own TV. Kat went along with her.

Alba lingered long enough to beg for comparisons between her food and Kat's, but I wasn't going there, so I straddled the fence and cast an indecisive vote.

With the girls all scattered back home, I put on my pajamas, turned on a fan of white noise, and sat cross-legged on my bed. I reached in the bedside table drawer. Finally, I could open the envelope I had received in the mail earlier. I felt a sort of dread and excitement combined. It was from Aunt El. I studied the artistically printed return address: Ellie Birdsong, Wayward, Georgia. With the exception of Aunt El, there was little in Wayward that I wanted to remember. I pulled open the tightly glued envelope and reached inside. At first I felt only the soft padding of cotton, then the cold feel of chain. I pulled out the necklace. Just as I suspected, it was the Alabama Crystal. Some long lost ancestor had picked it up in Montana on a healing journey. No one in the family remembers exactly what his ailment was, never mind his name, but they remember the quartz crystal because of the Obligation.

According to the story, a shaman had used the healing properties of the stone on my ancestor. Unfortunately, once his chakra had been balanced and his energies cleansed, said ancestor had "accidentally" stolen the crystal by packing it carefully in the hollow bottom of his boot and skipping town. The shaman was enraged and followed him back to Alabama, where he demanded the return of his crystal. In a mellow, moonshine mood, my ancestor repented and offered his own crystal liquor to the shaman. Appeased by this reimbursement and, ultimately, quite drunk, the shaman extended his show of good will by releasing guardianship of the crystal to his new friend.

He was, however, very clear about the Obligation. The one who possessed the crystal also possessed the ability to heal ailments, cleanse spirits, and prevent terrible choices in love. It was the Obligation of the owner to never use the love choice preventive but once in their lifetime. They could, however, pass it on in their bloodline or to a favored friend.

Personally, I had yet to see anyone that I could prove had used it. Everyone in our family appeared undeniably poor. A good love choice would have been someone with a bit of money. My grandparents both worked their farm. It was fifty acres of prime land, but they never seemed to have a spare nickel. My grandfather believed that storms waited patiently for his crops to grow just so they could destroy them. He held little faith in the crystal. My grandmother, on the other hand, loved the crystal. She adored her husband and daughters and felt the crystal had given her the gift of a love that conquers all. Whether they believed in the crystal or not, the family held fast in the belief that the Obligation was nothing to be scoffed at. It was taken seriously.

My mother had been the first to string it on a chain. The ritual of wrapping it in deer skin and folding it into a safe place had not appealed to her active lifestyle. She possessed a fast mind and her body was always scurrying to keep up. By the time my mother received the crystal from her mother, it had acquired the energy signatures of quite a few souls. My mother held it gingerly between her fingers and promptly ordered a gold chain.

Ours was a vague family at times in terms of relationships. My grandmother had produced two daughters, my mother, Lily, and her sister, Ellie. Ellie was the oldest. She had met Reuben Birdsong when she went to town for a work suit shortly after graduation. She planned to be a secretary in the city. Apparently Reuben swept her off her feet. He was working on water lines with a construction crew. They saw each other secretly for a long while, but things turned serious after she discovered she was two months pregnant. Reuben lived somewhere on a reservation. He never mentioned the location. He married Ellie a few days after she announced her pregnancy. On the day the baby was born, he grasped the small bundle in both arms and extended her to the sky. While the women were busily preparing Aunt El to nurse the baby, Reuben walked away, baby and all. It was the tragedy of Aunt El's life, losing that child.

No one had anything to offer the police but a description of Reuben. No one knew where he came from or where he went with the baby. Everyone had assumed there would be time for all the facts later. The main focus had been on the pregnancy. Aunt El never married again and had no other children. When she married Reuben, she had been presented with the Alabama Crystal. After her tragic loss, the crystal was passed to my mother, with Aunt El stating she never wanted to lay eyes on it again.

In a family of strong, plain women, my mother was an enigma of beauty and weakness. Aunt El was ten years older and, as a child, was charged to set a good example. She made a valiant attempt on all fronts, right down to dressing her younger sibling, dragging out her sewing kit and creating a purple frock dress that was so appealing that even her own mother was stunned. She treated little Lily like the manger child of Wayward, Georgia. She carried Lily on her small hip, rocked her, fed her, and, later on, fought all her battles with a vengeance. Lily was nine years old when Reuben took off with Aunt El's baby. The loss of her child and the total helplessness of the authorities in finding any evidence of Reuben's existence took a hard toll. Everyone feared Aunt El might die of grief. Everyone but Lily worried excessively. Lily was not about to have any rocks pulled from her support system. She flung herself into charming Aunt El back from the dull, lifeless place she had hidden. When charm failed, she attacked by dropping to the floor one morning with a dull thud. She tossed and turned on her bed in a fake -fever of delirium. Aunt El brushed her golden curls back with fear and horror. She begged her to recover. Lily tossed a few more days, whispering "Ellie" in a frail, sad voice. Aunt El created every dish she could imagine and recited the child's favorite stories interspersed with pleading gasps of desperation. Lily's distraction worked perfectly: Aunt El shaped up and refocused on her original commitment.

Ellie and Lily lost their parents shortly after the loss of Ellie's baby in an explosion at the church. The basement boiler had been bad for years but the church was trying to squeeze it through another year before making repairs. Ellie assumed all responsibility for Lily and worked as a seamstress at home to support them both.

When Lily was seventeen, a serendipitous encounter sent her from Wayward. Her sister needed a thimble for her latest sewing project and sent Lily to the store. As she was walking by the bus station she noticed a tall dark haired man in sunglasses leaning against the building. He seemed to be watching something, but it was impossible to tell through the dark lenses. Lily was wearing a skin tight green sleeveless shirt and a gray skirt. She felt oddly hot and uncomfortable as she watched the man. She loved his stance and the cool, blowsy look of his white shirt and pants. She loved how his brown jaw line seemed above the human frailties of sweat and fatigue. When a bus pulled in with Atlanta written above the windshield, she asked the driver to wait while she hurried in and bought a ticket. By the time the Greyhound reached Atlanta, Lily and the stranger, Briar Taylor, were best of friends. By the time they left Atlanta three days later, they were also best of lovers.

Briar was rich. This was a fact he revealed a week or so after the bus ride, when Lily realized her spending money and the thimble money had spent out. She took to this new facet of her life instantly. If it was possible for her love and passion for Briar Taylor to reach new heights, this statement did it. He was the son of generations of money, had just finished college, and his family was indulging his rest and reward period before he was introduced to balancing the books. He had a vague plan of touring Europe. Lily liked the plan but not the vagueness. She swiftly took things in hand and secured tickets to Italy. All she knew of Italy was the little she had read in school and some comments her well-traveled English teacher had made. Apparently it was a place of beauty, hot blooded men, and huge pots of pasta. That was enough for her.

On the flight over she gagged with fear and nearly suffocated from claustrophobia. She hid her face in Briar's shoulder a great deal. She loved the way he bent and cuddled her, doing his best to offer comfort. His dark hair falling over his forehead, his eyes green as grass and full of mirth, he made up stories to distract her thoughts from the emptiness beneath them. The trip seemed endless and the landing shaky, but Lily loved Italy instantly. Their destination, Volterra, was a hillside city, brimming with life. The centuries had left an unusual display of architecture to be admired. She was in awe of the landscape and hillside housing. She loved the colors, the passion, and the clothes. Briar, in turn, loved to watch her excitement as she roamed from store to store. They rented a suite of rooms and ordered delicious food from the gold gilted menu. It was a happy time.

Lily wrote Ellie for the first time three weeks after she arrived in Italy.

She told her all about Briar: his sweetness, their great love, his passion for spaghetti, and his money. Ellie wrote a heartbreaking answer filled with pleas for her return to Wayward, and shock at her sudden disappearance. She had been worried sick about Lily after someone – she never remembered who, the shock was so great – came forward and revealed having seen her on a Greyhound bus with a strange man. Lily wrote back and told her it was definitely love, a meeting of soul mates. She also mentioned that she thought she was pregnant. She said it was something she sensed in her spirit.

When I was born nine months later, my parents were still being indulged. Ellie was indulgent because she had no choice; Briar's parents because they had no idea that Briar was up to anything more than a wild oats bachelor period. Lily had sailed through pregnancy. She had enjoyed the dark women, fascinated by her beauty and child-like ways, who had catered to her at the hotel. They were equally enthralled with her baby, which left her plenty of time to recover. Briar was also fascinated with the baby. He named her Sylvia, after a friend in college. She had brown eyes. Lily said her mother had eyes the same color.

Since Sylvia was a quiet baby and was often carried away to markets and festivals by the women, he decided she was no problem. Things went very well for a while. Then Lily discovered she was pregnant again. She breezed through the nine month gestation once more physically, but emotionally things were changing. Briar had developed an interest in the local musicians. He made friends with many of them and began leaving large tips for their performances.

With her second child, Lily grew huge and cumbersome. She also developed a passion for sleep. She wrote Ellie that she was sleeping her life away. Briar was puzzled by her lack of enthusiasm for life, but distracted by his jovial new friends. When Lily finally gave birth, it was with a sigh of relief. The new baby, Katherine, was lovely. She was nicknamed Kat for her large cat-like green eyes and sharp features. The women in Lily's life took this child to their bosoms as well. Lily was once more able to attend parties with Briar. Now her sleepiness disappeared into a wild round of social events. The musicians were their best friends. They decided to travel with them and leave the babies with the women they'd grown to trust. Lily bought the women lovely dresses and left a great deal of cash with them for the care of her babies. She and Briar set off across the countryside, but their car overturned at a steep drop off. Lily, Briar, and the musicians were all killed. When the women received word at the hotel, they contacted Ellie for instructions. Ellie contacted Briar's parents.

They were stunned and grief stricken, but unable to believe Briar had two children in another country. They refused to help with the children, other than to arrange for their travel to Wayward. Ellie tried to contact them for several years afterwards but always met with a dead wall of silence. It was as if, for them, Briar and all associated with him had ceased to exist.

Chapter Two

I awakened the next morning with the Alabama Crystal in my hand. I shoved it quickly into the nightstand drawer and jumped up and headed for the shower. Katie was in crisis again. Her sister, Mandy, had arrived unexpectedly from Florida and needed a place to stay. For most people it would not be a problem, but Katie was torn between letting her stay and body slamming her into the next state. Kat and I were cheering for the next state scenario, but Katie had a heart bigger, and was willing to forgive just about anyone's transgressions. And, believe me, transgressions abounded with Mandy. She was two years younger than Katie, the baby in a family of five girls. A family ruled by the iron fist of a tough mama. All the girls clung closely to home, with the exception of Katie and Mandy. At thirteen, Katie had been expelled to the streets after being caught in a compromising sexual position. She wandered those streets before being taken up by an older man. Personally, I always felt the mama had an unjust jealousy of Katie. But what do I know.

Katie was naturally tall and lean with golden skin and bright blue eyes. Her hair was a thick, shiny blonde that she enhanced with yellow highlights. She had been married three times by the time she was twenty-five. She was unfailingly kind and always ready to defend a just cause.

This natural tendency toward compassion was what defeated her common sense in regard to Mandy, not to mention the poorly chosen men in her life. Although Katie had been shoved from the house and forbidden to return, the same transgressions had earned Mandy a protective love from the tough mama. Perhaps it was because Mandy was Mama's mirror image. Mandy was small, dark haired, and fair skinned, with a tendency toward chronic illness. She worked the room and the world with it. A doctor had diagnosed her with a multiple personality disorder. She was fifty-two people in one. I kind of thought that was improbable, and that she used each "personality" as needed to get her way, obtain whatever she wanted. She had a fixation on following Katie and stealing her men. First she would give a distress phone call, followed by her sickly arrival, followed by a blush of good health until whatever man Katie was with had been seduced. Anyway, this was the problem we were pondering. Kat suggested the Salvation Army.

Katie rolled her eyes and said, "She's my sister."

"Right!" Kay replied, "with an army of personalities especially designed for your destruction."

Katie was uncertain. She had a new boyfriend named Igor. Long brown hair, muscular build, and a longing to play guitar in a big band. Of course, he had to learn to play first. And he needed a guitar. He lived with her and had actually sought employment a couple of times a week. He was a winner.

"Sylvia," she asked, "do you think I should let her stay?" I hated being put on the spot. Of course, my first thought was to suggest she share her home with a couple of big poisonous vipers, but I could see she was already working on that. I could also see my opinion meant nothing, really, and that she was just killing time to avoid Kat's disapproval.

I went with the weak, sniveling approach.

"She *is* your sister," I said. Kat shot me a look of disgust. She crooked her arm and bent as though walking with a cane. It was her mime-type depiction of lame. I laughed. It *was* a lame answer.

"I'm going into town," I said. "I'll let you two figure out the Mandy situation." Kat flung her arm out and pretended to catch herself while falling to the floor.

While Kat and Katie were searching for solutions for their problem, I was searching for my own. My car was nearing the last stages of death, and I was trying to put off the grief process by visiting the local mechanic, Billy Mac. The old wreck was a screaming banshee of age and car aches when I pulled up to the wide open doors. Billy Mac continued talking to a customer while motioning me on in. I tried to straddle the pit perfectly with my car and sighed with relief when the tires hit gently against the iron stops. Billy Mac walked over and stood in front of me with his arms crossed. I could tell he dreaded asking what the problem was. My previous visits and car sound explanations always made him sigh. I decided to go with a verbal identification of the problem.

"My car sounds like a wounded cow. It screams and shakes. Sometimes it follows up with a high pitched screech!"

Billy Mac waited a moment to reply. He wanted to be certain that I was not going to follow up with additional dramatics.

He said, "Let me take a look. You can wait inside."

I went in and perched lightly on the greasy chair before picking up an oily magazine. All I could hear was the scream and whine of some sort of machine nearby. It was like a mechanical, off-key opera. Fifteen minutes later Billy Mac was standing in front of me again, this time wiping his hands on a dirty red cloth and shaking his head.

"I know the problem now," he said. I was all ears, but obviously he was waiting for some sort of response.

"What is it?" I asked, simply enough.

"Your axle is going. Lucky you made it here. You're riding in a death trap."

Hmmm, I thought, now who's being dramatic? But to him I said, "Can you fix it, and how much?"

He grinned, "I can fix anything, baby. Come on into my office."

I followed him in, thinking how loosely the word office applied here. I saw a small cot, a coffee maker, and what appeared to be a hand-thrown attempt to decorate with nuts and bolts. He shut his office door and dropped his pants.

"Whoa," I said, trying for humor, "it's a little cold today to work in the nude."

"I do my best work naked," he said happily.

"Wait a second!" I said. But it was too late. I heard a low steady hum and actually gawked in amazement. It was a mechanical penis, rising to the occasion at slow speed.

"See this?" he said, as if I could see anything else. "I just hit this little switch here and it stays up as long as it's needed."

"Well," I said, as always in crisis, falling back on politeness, "it is certainly something to see. It's, um, quite something," I continued, stepping back a few feet, my head cocked to the side in what I hoped was a studious position, as I reached for the door behind me, flung it open, and fled. Needless to say, my death trap car felt like a magic carpet as I rumbled backwards out of the garage and down the road.

"Crap," I said, "he was the cheapest and best mechanic in town!" Then, of course, my mind wandered back to the mechanical penis. I made it home in half the time it usually took.

Later that week, I took the car to Sears and shopped while the axle was replaced. On the way home I stopped at the post office. I had plenty of bills and one letter from Darrie Demar at the county jail. She said she would be out of jail just in time for a Friday night gathering at the round table. She also said she had a new boyfriend that was innocently incarcerated, someone she'd met in the men's compound. He was a trustee and she passed notes to him with the assistance of a mutual friend, also incarcerated, also innocent. Of course.

I knew the girls would be happy to see Darrie. She was a sweet trusting soul in her mid-forties to whom we had given a ride to a few years before. She had been wrestling a local grocery store's cart down Main Street heading for the laundromat with a load of clothing. The sleeves of work shirts flapped in the wind and appeared to be waving in response to the cool stares of pedestrians. We picked her up because she looked desperate. Her hair was prematurely grey. Her eyes were grey, warm, and crinkling happily. She said she was down on her luck since her husband had died suddenly from a diabetic coma.

We took her to the laundromat and left, but on the way back through town we noticed she was just starting back up Main Street, so we took her home. She invited us all in for pretzels and Coke and a tarot card reading. We had been her only friends since then, with the exception of the boyfriends that came and went with the weather. Anyway, it would be nice to see her again Friday.

I also stopped to grab some yeast for Alba at the health food store. Before I could make it out of the store, she called and added a request for a sage stick. I told her I had sage left over from Thanksgiving, but she said, "No, it's a twisted bundle of sage I need to cleanse my house with." It seemed a little crazy to me but I asked the shopkeeper and he brought out the bundled sticks. I paid for the purchase, and headed for home. I knew Kat would want to know that I had the Alabama Crystal, but I planned to give things a bit more thought before I mentioned it to her.

Katie dropped by, depressed. She had discovered that Mandy had made a move on Igor, who had responded poorly, in Katie's mind, by taking her to bed. Since Katie had no choice but to forgive her constantly unstable sister, she had kicked Igor out.

"That didn't take long," Kat said.

"I know," Katie said. She had her hands up rubbing each side of her head in circular motions.

"Do you think I reacted too hastily," Katie asked.

"What do you mean," Kat asked. "Do I think you should have let him have a few more fun moments with Mandy? Not hardly."

"Now I don't have anyone," Katie said sadly.

"I am sorry, Katie. You deserve the best, but even you have to admit that Igor wasn't the best. That name alone is a turn off to me. People that change their names to their favorite kid movie character may have other problems."

"I know," Katie said, "but, you know, it will be hard to find another musician."

"You haven't found the first one yet," Kat said. "Igor found one chord and hung onto it like a leech, tormented it against its will, and then held on until it died a terrible tone death."

"I'm so angry at Mandy, Kat. Why does she do these things? I mean, I guess I know why, but it's so hard to deal with," Katie said.

"I know," Kat responded, "and I'm sorry. I don't know the answer. At least you know that she doesn't do it to hurt you. She does it because she wants to be like you. Strong, whole, and kind."

Even though she wanted to hate Mandy, we all knew that Katie would make up with her, so there wasn't a whole lot of point in being mean about it. Mandy only wanted to do the things that Katie did. Unfortunately, she also wanted to do the same men. If Katie liked them, they were more than good enough for Mandy. Mandy also suffered a great paranoia of men. She would never stay very long with one, but grow increasingly restless, finally changing personalities and making a run for it. I felt very badly for Katie. She had such a beautiful heart. It was not just Mandy that she forgave time and time again, but her parents, the men in her life, co-workers. She was always giving out fresh starts – and beginning them, also. She was a burned phoenix, rising again and again to stick the pieces of her heart together with a super glue made of time.

Chapter Three

As Lily's body was lowered into a plot at the family cemetery, Ellie stood in dull grief, one baby in her arms, the other clutching her hand. The Alabama humidity blended with the tears on her face. A terrible grief for her bright and beautiful Lily combined with an overwhelming sense of responsibility and survival. The children were beautiful and quiet. They were used to being passed among the affectionate Italian women and adjusted well to their new guardian. Ellie prepared Lily's old room as a nursery. She hung pink hand-sewn curtains at the window and draped the bed with a canopy, which the wind through the open window caressed in a warm, soft flow. Ellie only had a small amount of the money left from her parents. She worked four days a week at home sewing for the ladies in town. Her skill with the needle was unmatched. She also cleaned rooms at the retirement center in town two days a week. Sunday was reserved for church.

The first night with the babies, Ellie sat up watching them sleep. They were like beautiful princesses beneath the elegant canopy. Their complexions had the soft pink glow of the inside of a seashell. Their small perfect features fascinated her. She felt a deep love and protectiveness toward them. Their hands lay so small and open in vulnerable innocence. When she finally grew tired, she rested on the sofa so she could watch through the doorway and hear them easily if they awakened. Ellie's longing to see Lily was so intense she felt physically ill. To never again look upon that beloved face, to never see her sister's mischievous smile again filled her soul with despair. She dreamed that night of Lily and the Alabama Crystal.

The next morning she searched through Lily's things. There, at the bottom of the suitcase, in a small box she found the crystal. She loved the fact that Lily had added the gold chain. She enjoyed knowing that Lily had worn it close to her heart. Ellie wasn't sure if anyone other than she, herself, had ever used the crystal. She knew Lily had probably never used it, just as their mother had never used it. It could only be used once by each owner. As far as she knew, no one had ever considered the legend true, nor tried to demand a performance. Still, no one in the family for generations had considered doing anything to incur the wrath of the shaman by treating the crystal with disrespect. Ellie came from a long line of superstitious people. Her own usage of the crystal during the brief time she used it was to ask for a safe birth for her baby. She had to admit the baby was born safely, but where was she now? Was she safe now? The thought of her baby sent her hurrying back to the new babies. Sylvia and Katherine were waking up. She took them into the kitchen to prepare breakfast. Ellie had pulled a little table and chair from the attic that had once belonged to Lily, and it in the open doorway. Sylvia sat quietly in her little chair. The sun danced bright shadows across the porch. She reached out to catch them. Ellie held Kat and rocked her. Kat pulled at her bottle with perfect cherubic lips as she stared upwards into Ellie's face. Ellie thought she looked confident and certain. Suddenly, she felt the same way. She could do this.

Chapter Four

I lit a couple of odd-shaped fragrant candles and placed them on the table. The girls would be here any minute. It should be an interesting night. Alba called and said she would be over in five minutes. She had to finish cleansing. She was cleansing her way out the back door now. God knows what she was cleansing, but I do not. She lived alone, her house was immaculate, and she was allergic to pets. I imagine some bad odor off the street had drifted in. Alba was very spiritual. She would take any odd smell for a communicating spirit. I knew she would be happy to see Darrie, because Darrie was a walking fountain of information regarding love and woe. Unfortunately, somewhere along the line, someone had passed her a pair of non-removable rose colored glasses. She was completely unaware of her bad luck and had an amazing ability to twist everything into a good omen.

Kat and Katie were riding together. Kat was supposed to be Katie's moral support. They had picked up Mandy at the bus station thirty minutes ago, and were en route, ETA any second. Mandy was the reason Katie needed moral support, of course. Katie was uneasy about having all those personalities in one room. Mandy was so skinny, I couldn't conceive of her hosting so many others inside herself, but so it goes, I guess. It was really beyond not only my ken, but my interest, except as it affected Katie. I still held to my opinion that Mandy was a consummate actress, not a multiple personality at all.

Alba arrived first. She had cooked up some fine smelling banana bread in the midst of all that cleansing. Kat walked in with Katie and Mandy a few minutes later. Kat opened her container and placed it on the table beside of Alba's. I shifted uneasily. It was banana bread. Kat was a champion baker of moist, delightful banana bread. So was Alba. I could see I would be stuffed by the end of the night trying to keep the amount missing from the containers at an equal portion. If either of them ended up with one more piece than the other, it was a slap of failure.

Everyone seated themselves while I poured coffee and placed a cup in front of each of them. Mandy waved hers away and stated that she'd prefer a cup of yogurt. "You may, indeed," I said, a little uneasy about the date on it. There are lots of good things to eat in the world.

There was a large chance that the yogurt had been with me longer than most of the other edibles. I handed over a chocolate yogurt, but she was skeptical of her digestive tract. I replaced it with a strawberry flavor and pretended not to hear her put-upon sigh. Anything could create a martyr state with Mandy. She pulled a thousand crosses behind her when she crossed a room. Even seated, she managed to create an essence of being a thin vulnerable package of humanity. She kept a shawl around her shoulders, wore over-sized clothing, and always conveyed the feeling that she was next in line for execution. Everyone was relieved to hear Darrie shout, "Knock, knock!" from the doorway. We all rushed to give her a hug.

"It is so wonderful to see all of you," she beamed as she took a seat. I poured her the last of the coffee. "Wait until you hear what happened to me," she said excitedly, as though she had just returned from some fine vacation and couldn't wait to give details. She grabbed a piece of Alba's banana bread. I grabbed a piece of Kat's. She waved her bread like a crumb baton as she spoke. "Well, when I realized that the money orders Eddie kept writing so freely spelled trouble, I was just sick! I wasn't even aware a person could make up a money order. Thank God I didn't cash any of his traveler checks! Six months in jail just for believing in that man! Still, if it hadn't been for the time spent there, I would never have met Chuck. Chuck is short for Charles! I guess I'm just naturally lucky. Just plain lucky!" Darrie tended to talk in exclamation points, every sentence being excitement-ridden. Katie perked up instantly at the reference to luck. She believed in the powers of luck and karma. She also had quite a few jailhouse romances under her belt.

Alba was listening intently but cutting her eyes occasionally toward the banana bread. I was listening to Darrie but distracted and just a little fascinated by Mandy. She was taking tiny bites of yogurt and chewing them slowly and carefully. I had never seen anyone chew yogurt, especially when it had no fruit in it.

Darrie said, "One day a trustee named Jackson came by with a note. It was from his cell mate, Chuck Owens. We started sending notes by Jackson each day and love just bloomed. It grew like a wild flower! I felt sorry for Jackson. He kept asking if I knew anyone he could write to, or anyone that might visit. I thought of you, Katie!"

Katie beamed proudly, "I may already know him. I know an Alan Jackson."

"That's him!" Darrie squealed. "They caught him on camera filling up his truck with gas and driving off. Of course, it wasn't him. He said anyone with eyes could see that his truck was a deeper red. I don't see how three gas stations could be so wrong. He said if he had been appointed a better lawyer he could have beat them and proved himself innocent. Anyway, you should write him, Katie. He's a real sweet guy! But let me finish about Chuck. He isn't in there for anything violent. He has this awful ex-wife that dogs him for child support constantly. He said that three of the five kids don't even belong to him. He said that he tried in every way to appease the courts, but he didn't make enough to pay month after month, at the exact time they told him to pay. He works on roofs and some months it's impossible to get out to work because of the weather. You know it's impossible to put a roof on in the winter."

"That's true," Kat said. "And God forbid a tough construction guy look for an inside job!" Darrie nodded in agreement, but a slight frown crossed her face. For a moment I thought she might actually consider why a man wouldn't work inside to support his family, but she shook it off and continued.

"You should see his body. I can just picture him shirtless on the roof, sweating in the hot sun. Anyway, when he gets out we plan to live together. He will need a place to stay and it's so lonely by myself. He's going to help me with the bills. I'm so glad Daddy left me our family home. I have a job already as a shampooer at Cut It Cute. I plan to give you girls a discount!"

We all thanked her politely. She was getting ready to render her description of Chuck when a wail rang out. We all jumped and looked at Mandy. She was perched on the edge of her chair, stripped down to a halter top and panties. Her hair was twisted over one shoulder and her eyes wide and seductive. "It es hot in here," she said.

"Oh, no," Katie moaned, "that's her slut personality! Her name is Liz."

"How can you tell?" Kat asked innocently as she bent double laughing.

"Shh, don't upset her," Katie said.

I wasn't sure what to say. Maybe it was the yogurt, or maybe a picture of Chuck shirtless on the roof had slipped past her mild-mannered "normal" self to activate the inner Liz. She seemed ready to seduce her chair at the moment.

"Who vants to party with Liz?" she asked in an absurd, trying-to-be-coy French lisp.

"I hate that personality," said Katie bitterly. "That's the one that seduced all my men."

"I think we should take her out on the town," Darrie said.

"I think we should nominate her for the Academy Awards," Kat said.

"Let's take her home," Katie said. "She doesn't know what is happening when a personality takes over."

Suddenly Mandy grabbed her pants and pulled them on roughly. She stood wide-legged and stiff. "What the hell is going on here," she said in a gruff voice. Then she turned to Darrie and said, "Baby, you want to see some sweat?" She pulled off her halter top.

"Oh, no," Katie said. "That's Bill! He's a roofer, too!"

Mandy had our full attention now. We wanted to see more of the man personality. I wanted to see what she had to say as a man. Kat suggested she hook up with Liz.

"Who the hell is Liz?" Mandy/Bill asked slyly.

"Hey, can you sing," Darrie asked eagerly, "We could go to the karaoke bar!"

"I do duets," Mandy/Bill said.

"Well, I'll do one with you!" she said.

"I only do 'em with Patsy!" s/he growled.

Katie said in a stage whisper, "Patsy is another personality. She sings like a dream! I mean, she thinks she does. I haven't had the heart to tell her otherwise."

"It's my bedtime," I said, anxious for a way out. "You guys have been fun, but I have to turn in. I have Mrs. Crank tomorrow." On weekends I tried to make a little extra income at the nursing home. Mrs. Crank paid me privately to visit her.

The girls all left, probably headed for the bar to celebrate Darrie's release and to let Mandy express her selves in song. I put the cups in the sink and went to bed. Mrs. Crank liked me to arrive at six a.m. on the dot.

She had a variety of pranks she enjoyed playing on the other residents; all of them harmless, most of them fun.

Chapter Five

The next morning I arrived at the nursing home at six. The nurses were annoyed that I called it a nursing home. They liked to identify it as a retirement village. I don't know what the difference is, but Mrs. Crank insisted that it be called a nursing home, especially if her son or daughter showed up. It annoyed them; it annoyed the nurses, too, but it pleased Mrs. Crank. She liked to bring up the fact that her children refused to live with her, thus causing her sad relocation to the nursing home. She paid five hundred dollars a weekend, every weekend, for me to show up and bring her gifts. She even purchased the gifts herself through me. She would choose things from the catalogs she subscribed to, then have me order them with her Visa. I was to bring them as gifts each Saturday morning. This drove the son and daughter mad with jealousy. They feared I was trying to buy her love. Their concern amused Mrs. Crank. I think she hoped that jealousy would drive them to visit more often.

Mrs. Crank had tons of money. It would have been easier for her to stay in her own home and hire a companion, but her mansion was located in the country and she enjoyed living in town now. She also enjoyed the nursing home, since she was extremely popular with the residents. In the '30s she had been a successful model for department stores, and still maintained a regal walk, and her thick, smooth cap of now-white hair. Although pretending to be cool and above it all, Mrs. Crank was a keen judge of character. She was also very kind, and enjoyed giving anonymously to the other residents who were without family or friends. She was popular with the men due to both her past career and present regality. She was popular with the women for her patience in taking time to read them their mail, should any arrive. She had a wonderful sense of humor and loved practical jokes. Often she used my services to place a large pile of banana peels in the middle of the hallway. Of course, she insisted I let no real harm happen, but she loved to watch the reactions of the residents. I would stand at the end of the hallway and tell her which resident would be approaching. The banana pile was reserved for the grouchy souls with no sense of humor whatsoever. They would approach slowly, paying no heed until they were within a few feet. She loved their expressions of outrage and their bells. All of the residents carried bells in case of emergency, and it delighted Mrs. Crank to hear one ring furiously. When the hapless victim of her practical joke turned to look and see if anyone was heeding their ringing, I would swiftly remove the peels to Mrs. Crank's room.

She drove the cook crazy by pasting pictures of a Nazi refugee camp victims on the door that led to the kitchen. She placed fake poop in the visitor's area when it was time for the inspectors. All in all, she was an odd, but charming woman. Although Mrs. Crank often acted aggrieved by her children, she harbored a great devotion to them. Her son was very successful in banking and her daughter was a dress designer. Both children were devoted to her, which was why they were so upset that she not only signed herself into the home and blamed them, but that she blatantly refused to live with either of them. They suffered extreme guilt, as good children often do, and longed for her to be pleased with them. Mrs. Crank thought that guilt would make them stronger. She did not want to live with them, but she did want them to want her to.

We spent most of the day talking and rearranging her picture albums. I had purchased stickers with comments on them to put with the pictures. Under a lovely shot of her with a fur off the shoulder, I placed the word, "Ooh-la-la!"

"That may be a tad too vain, dear," she said.

"No," I said, "this is definitely an 'ooh-la-la' shot!" She seemed pleased and began looking for a word to paste under her husband's photo. I waited patiently. Finally she found the right one and I glued it on for her. "Stud."

"Wow," I said, "that's a good word for a husband."

"A true word also," she said. "He was quite a man. He was smitten with love from the moment he lay eyes on me."

"Of course," I said.

She completed one book and began another. This one held beautiful photos of her children. We used the hearts and stars to decorate their pictures. She kept one book of photos to herself. I respected her privacy. I told her about the night before. She was always interested in the Friday night meetings. She loved the fact that Mandy had mutiple personalities and begged me to bring her to visit. I told her I couldn't promise, but would try. I was tired when I left the home. I enjoyed my work, and Mrs.

Crank was entertaining, with a spark of life about her that made others want to blaze, too. However, some of the others were terribly heartbreaking. One lady, Mary, had been placed in the home against her will. Her sister, Beth, had fallen, and the ladies' nephew had asked Mary to ride along when he admitted Beth. Secretly, he had admitted both. It took a very long time and plenty of sedation for Mary to adjust. She stayed faithfully with her sister in the end, but the freedom that was taken from her enraged me. There were many others that were admitted under the same sort of false pretenses, and I felt it was an ultimate betrayal on the part of their families. It is a terrible thing to be forgotten, and many of them were. Of course, there were families that had no choice, and others that visited faithfully and tenderly cared for their aging parents. These were the ones that renewed my hope in love and compassion.

As soon as I arrived home, I slipped into something more comfortable, which, in my case, is a long soft linen shirt and a pair of terry cloth shorts. I curled up on the couch to read. I had ordered a collection of books by Taylor Caldwell, and was browsing through to see if I could find any I hadn't read before. I love Caldwell. Her writing career began when she was twelve, no small feat in and of itself, and her insights into human nature, even at that young age, were remarkable.

Then I remembered a package of books I had received earlier in the week but had been forced to put aside and then forgotten. It contained several books about the life of Edgar Cayce, the Virginia Beach psychic. I loved his theories on reincarnation and the revolving journeys of the soul toward perfection. Just as I located the package, I heard the back door open.

"It is just me," Alba said, "I have the Sunday blues. Would you like to share some Cherry Yum Yum?"

"I could force myself," I kidded. "I *am* starving. Where are your blues coming from? Do you have a secret passion I'm unaware of that's left you lingering in despair?"

"Hardly," she said dryly. "Just a house that reeks with silence. Sometimes silence is tranquil, but this one could bore the dead."

I laughed and confessed to having the same feeling. She collapsed into a chair while I grabbed plates and forks from the cabinet.

"Some days I feel so alone," she said. "I wish that I had a huge family that kept me constantly entertained and cooking. If I did, I'd be preparing a huge Sunday dinner right now, and soon everyone would be fighting over the last biscuit at the dinner table."

"Wow, you *are* lonely," I said. "Think of all those dishes. I'm pretty sure everyone would excuse themselves quickly once the food was gone."

She laughed and said, "This is my fantasy; please keep all negative opinions out of it."

"And then there are all those events! Pregnancies, wedding showers, parties," I said. "And that would be fun, except there would be someone, some snippy, never-happy relative, who would believe you'd added too much salt to the potato salad."

"And I would tell that person what to do with it," she said indignantly, already a bit peeved at this imaginary relative and his or her snide remarks on her cooking skills. I enjoyed Alba's quick temper, once again flaring so rapidly out of her demure, prim posture.

"Oh," I said, "and lots of little ones. Adorable small children gently grasping a perfectly split deviled egg that would then be smeared from one end of your lovely sofa to the other. Or the other delightful little ones, using your rakes, hoes and shovels as spears and battle lances, accidently breaking them—not to mention themselves—with their rough-housing."

Alba was quite proud of her sofa, and she handled her gardening tools carefully.

"Why, I'd discipline them on the spot," she cried in outrage.

"No," I said sadly, "it wouldn't be possible. What I failed to mention is these children are perfect and angelic in the eyes of their parents. Fine, golden offspring left to wreak havoc, and woe to the woman who mentions their indiscretions!"

"Woe to the parents of those hellions," she said heatedly. "I simply would not tolerate it for a second. Why, if children aren't taught basic courtesy, their entire lives are affected. Lack of restraint and a failure to teach discipline destroys the spirit."

"But what if all the parents believe that the spirits of the children might be broken by restraint?"

"Are the parents insane? A lack of restraint builds a premise for the children that the world is theirs for the demanding. There is no respect or guilt, and without those two things, there is no conscience."

"This Yum Yum is incredible," I said. "Thank you."

"I'll leave it here in case the girls come by," she said. "I think I'll go home and work on the Sunday cross-word."

"Silence is probably still lurking around," I reminded her.

"Let him lurk," she said, "as long as he doesn't break anything." Then she smiled and headed home.

Chapter Six

It was peaceful growing up with Aunt El. She made it appear as though we were great assets she had acquired. We very seldom left the property but Aunt El let us explore the attic and countryside freely. She had inherited fifty acres, so we had a great deal of territory to cover and occupy our time. She had a wonderful sense of fun that she asserted in idle moments. She was excellent at board games and impossible to beat at chess or checkers, although she generously taught us all her moves. Our lives were spent in activities in rhythm with the season. In winter, Aunt El took us sledding. It was difficult to convince her to join in, but she loved to pull canisters of chocolate from her large army coat to surprise us. In summer we lay in the meadow grasses nearby and made daisy chains. Aunt El had a fear of drowning, so she taught us to swim when we were very young. Her phobia sprang from a day, long ago, when she had taken Lily to picnic by the river. She had turned away for a moment to shake the old quilt she had with her into a soft square for them to sit upon. Then she heard a splash. The look of fear in Lily's eyes was sickening to see. Even worse was the fear Aunt El felt in having to be the savior. Then she had snapped out of it, yanked up the quilt, and threw one end to Lily. Her fear of water never left her.

She also taught us to sew, but we grew bored easily when indoors, so our considerably-less-than-accomplished sewing was abandoned rather quickly. Kat was better at it than I was, but for the most part we were outdoors. It seemed that the sun was always shining. Since we had never known our parents, we did not miss them. Aunt El spoke of our mother very often, and kept her picture on our nightstand. She was a beautiful stranger to us, so we called her the angel lady. She looked very much like the angels in the storybook Aunt El read to us at bedtime. We had a happy childhood and our teen years went well also. I was anxious for my sixteenth birthday because Aunt El had promised me the Alabama Crystal. She had stored it carefully in a small teakwood box. I was happily pondering ways to use it, but Aunt El cautioned me to wait until I was older. The day she finally presented it to me, I held it to the light. The pale yellow light bulb did nothing to enhance its color, so Aunt El suggested I take it outside. Outside it seemed to light up with all the surrounding colors of the landscape. I was very pleased. I loved the golden chain, for my mother had chosen it. Kat was happy for me, but a little envious. Aunt El assured her that she, too, would one day own the crystal, as we'd agreed I would pass it on to Kat on her wedding day.

***

After I graduated from high school, I decided to wait to attend college. Kat would be graduating the following year; I wanted us to start together. I found a part time job in town at the Dairy Delight, servicing tables. I also delivered sewing for Aunt El. One evening I was held over at work by a group of students lingering over their banana splits. By the time they left and I had finished cleaning the equipment for the next day, it was almost nine o'clock. Aunt El always went to bed by eight thirty. Kat and I usually read a while before turning in ourselves. I hoped that Kat would still be awake. My boss, Mr. Jacobs, dropped me off on the main road about a half mile from my house. I then took the dirt road that lead to our door. Since it was late, Mr. Jacobs offered to take me all the way, but I wanted to walk in the quiet, watch the stars, and inhale the honeysuckle that lay in fragrant tangles along the road. I had only walked a short distance when I realized I smelled smoke. I broke into a run, frantic. When the house came into view I could see the smoke pouring from our small kitchen window. I was sick with fear but plunged in through the front door. One side was burning fiercely, but in the other rooms the smoke was just clinging to the ceiling, slowly but surely lowering. I ran to Aunt El's room. She took the situation in instantly, as a heavy layer of smoke was hovering over her bed. The two of us continued to Kat's room. She stumbled out of bed with a look of horror and we all hurried out the back door. Standing in the starlight in her pale flannel gown, Aunt El looked fragile and filled with despair. I was too happy that we had all escaped to feel anything but great joy. It was like being born again. I could tell Kat felt the same way. Suddenly I remembered the crystal.

"The Alabama Crystal!" I cried. I made a move to enter the house but Aunt El suddenly looked anything but fragile.

She grabbed my arms and said, "Forget the crystal!"

"But the magic," I said.

Aunt El's face twisted with grief and rage. "There is no magic. Don't you understand? There is no magic!"

I did not understand, and I was very frightened. Aunt El never raised her voice, and the look on her face was alien and full of rage. I could see Kat was stunned also. Her large green eyes filled her face as she moved closer to my side. Aunt El broke into tears. Kat and I wrapped our arms around her. The three of us stood sobbing.

Suddenly I heard the sound of a motor. It was Mr. Jacobs. He had noticed the smell when he arrived home, only a short distance up the main road from where he'd dropped me off earlier. He had decided to come back just in case it was something besides a brush fire. He watched the flames with us a moment, then went to investigate. He told us he believed that a spark from the fire had gone up the chimney and fallen on the house.

"This house is very old. It wouldn't have taken much of a spark," he said, shaking his head. "But it was quite a house."

Mr. Jacobs lived with three widowed sisters, all of them over seventy. Since he barely had room enough for himself, taking us in was out of the question. He decided to take us into town and rent us a room for a week. He said that would give Aunt El time to settle things. When we arrived at the small bed and breakfast inn, the owner, Miss Tally, listened aghast as he and Aunt El related the details of the night. She could see that Aunt El was at the breaking point, so she shooed us off to a room as quickly as possible. The room held two beds, but the three of us fell asleep cuddled up together on one.

When I woke up the next morning, Kat was still sleeping. Aunt El was standing at a large floor length window, staring outside. She turned and smiled as I walked toward her. I lay my head on her shoulder for a moment.

"Sylvia," she said, "I couldn't have been more blessed than to have enjoyed you and Kat as my own children. I thank God that we made it out of that house alive. In that way, we are very fortunate, but we have suffered a big financial loss. All the money I had was in that house. Everything we own is gone."

"Please don't worry so much," I pleaded. "We have each other and we must have insurance, right?"

"Oh, Sylvia, we have each other, but I was never able to insure the house. Long ago I had insurance, but the bills accumulated so quickly."

Because of us, I thought sadly. Because she took in two little girls when she was barely making it on her own. It was very unfair.

"Sylvia, my sewing machine, my material, threads; it was my livelihood that went up in the flames. I can't think how to start over."

"Aunt El, this room has been paid up for a week. I have a job, and Kat and I are very strong. Everything will be okay, better than okay," I said with furious, if perhaps unfounded, determination.

Miss Tally had a good reputation and a spotless bed and breakfast. Her large, two story house offered four bedrooms for rent. One of them was used by the local pharmacist, Ed Billing, and one by Dora Wells, an artist. The other two rooms had stood vacant for a long while before our arrival. Miss Tally devoted herself to maintaining her house and garden. In the summer, vegetables were a steady source of income. In the winter she sold delicious pies and fine, fluffy cakes to the merchants in town. Her renters had been with her for many years, so financially she was in good shape.

She was a short, large bodied woman with lively, kind black eyes. She was an only child, never married, instead devoting her courtship years caring for her elderly parents. After their deaths, her loneliness had led her to rent out rooms. She loved the company of others and treated her renters as family.

While Aunt El was tidying the room upstairs I went down to see if I could be of any assistance to Miss Tally. She was leaning over a cutting board, pressing her weight into the dough.

"Good bread should have plenty of kneading," she said as a greeting when I approached her in the kitchen. "This bread was started by my mother before she died. I take a little piece of dough off of each batch of biscuits and add it to the next batch. That way there is a little history and a little memory each time I bake."

"Oh," I said, "so each time you bake bread, it is your mother baking with you?"

"Yes," she said. She nodded and smiled, pleased that I understood. "How is your aunt? Such a terrible tragedy. Even with insurance, there are just so many things you can't replace."

"There is no insurance," I said. Then I thought of the Alabama Crystal and sighed.

"Don't be down in the dumps now. You take this little piece here and make a batch of bread. Start yourself a history from this very moment." She placed a small bowl in front of me and I stirred the ingredients as she poured them in. She used buttermilk, a handful of lard, and a little water.

Before I put it in the oven, she pinched off a small piece and sealed it in a bowl, telling me, "This is for future making."

She asked me to have Aunt El and Kat come down for breakfast. Aunt El was still pretty shaken, so Ms. Tally invited the three of us to eat in the warm kitchen. After setting places for her renters, she returned to join us.

The smell of fresh bread filled the room. Our landlady pulled out homemade grape jam and butter. We drank milk and coffee. It was a delicious meal. After we had cleaned the dishes and put them away, Aunt El asked Miss Tally if she could be of assistance in any other area of the house. Miss Tally knew Aunt El's skill with a needle, so she asked if she would mind sitting with her as she mended a few things.

"Only if you let me help," Aunt El said. Miss Tally willingly agreed. Kat went outside to sit on the back steps. She loved the garden and volunteered at breakfast to harvest the tomatoes that were ripe. I told her that I needed to go back home and search for the Alabama Crystal.

Chapter Seven

I woke up Monday morning with Kat banging around in my kitchen. Forever, it seemed, we'd held a spare key to each other's houses. Kat could be as stealthy as her name implied, so apparently she wanted me awake.

"Just trying to find the coffee," she said as I drooped into a chair.

"It's in the red canister beside the coffee pot," I replied, raising an eyebrow.

She laughed, "Okay. Sorry. But I have to tell you about last Friday. I wish you could have been there. The personalities were flying out like hotcakes off a madman's grill! The Bill one stayed off and on throughout the night. He did a couple of duets with Patsy, until she was suddenly replaced with a set of twins, one of them 25, the other eight! One twin ordered tequila, the other one was drinking hot chocolate. Man, was Mandy ever sick!

"Darrie became best friends with Liz, because she loved her accent. She invited her over to spend the night, but then the twins showed up. I sang *Love Will Build A Bridge* with Katie and Darrie. Everybody loved us. Then the Bill and Patsy personalities stood up to sing *Islands in the Stream*. They demanded two microphones. By then, the whole crowd was so drunk that they applauded anything, so Bill and Patsy were happy. Then the little twin fell asleep on the dance floor, so we all decided to leave."

"You mean Mandy passed out?"

"Yep! Down like a bag of wet cement. All that hot chocolate and tequila, plus Bill's beer, was too much for her. Patsy was drinking coffee, but we were *not* about to make her a designated driver."

I laughed, but before I could say anything, I heard Alba behind me.

"It's a shame to let someone think they have multiple personalities!" she said. "Why do you encourage her?"

"We do not encourage anything," Kat said coldly, "Her doctor does that." Kat reached for her purse.

"Oh," she said, "I'm taking my empty baking pan. Yours is in the fridge, Alba, still half full of banana bread, so you may want to get it later." She was gone before Alba could reply.

"Did you not like my banana bread?" Alba asked testily.

"I loved it," I said swiftly, "but Darrie begged me to save half a pan for her, so I did."

"Oh," she said, "so she really liked mine that much?"

"Yep," I replied, "she said she was going to ask you to make her a loaf for her birthday."

Appeased, she returned to the previous subject of the personalities.

"I really do not believe she has 52 personalities. Why would the doctor say such a thing? A body has one soul and spirit. It must be nurtured and trained to serve the one true Great Spirit. It must be dedicated to that, and to the creations that are a gift to us."

"Okay," I said.

"Okay? What do you mean?"

"I mean I have no idea how to reply to your statements or questions. How can anyone reply to anything that is based on faith and belief? We all have our own version playing in our heads of what we believe to be true."

"I am trying to tell you the way now, Sylvia!"

"Yes, I know, but I don't know that you know the way."

"What is wrong with you," she demanded. "Can't you see how enlightened I am?"

"Yes, I can see that," I said. "I can also see Mandy's 52 personalities, personalities she believes to be real. I can see how one event in my life may have led into another, which may have been inspired by a guardian angel. I believed a man I saw howling at the moon when he said he believed it would howl back."

"I am not listening to much more of this," she said. "Look, a person has one soul and he or she must lift it up by faith."

"If I lifted by faith and you lifted by faith, would both faiths rise to the same height?"

"I *will* be back later," she said, huffing out of the kitchen, "Please tell Darrie to return my loaf pan as soon as she is able to do so."

As soon as she left, I locked the door. I liked Alba. She'd moved in shortly after I bought this house. I wasn't much on visiting, but Alba made it her goal to know her neighbors wherever she lived. She told me so the first visit. I didn't lean heavily either way on her neighborly theory but I was captivated by the pecan dark chocolate fudge. It sweetened things up between us a great deal. She dropped in so often that she soon became a fixture at the Friday night get togethers. What else could I do? The woman knew more about my routine than I did. If someone charged me with a crime and I had to prove my whereabouts, Alba would be the one to alibi me.

I no longer wanted to sleep; I wanted to clean house. I opened the blinds and the sunlight splashed off the pane. I was thinking of the Alabama Crystal again.

Chapter Eight

When I returned to look for the crystal in the ashes, the house was still smoldering. I could see black, charred lumps, and the twisted shapes of old furnishings. It was a melted mess, impossible to distinguish anything. I stood on the warm grass trying to decide where my room had once been. I walked to the side of the house and tried to decipher a more exact location. I used a large stick to lift and move the hot pieces. It took a long time to find the crystal.

Suddenly a prism of light flashed from the ashes. The chain was no longer there, but the crystal itself was intact. I felt a great relief and, at last, hope for the future. The crystal held all the dreams we had of starting our lives over. I knew I couldn't wait to use it. We were destitute. I sat down in the grass and rubbed the crystal clean with the end of my blouse. I used the crystal for the healing of my family. I closed my eyes and asked that fortune shine upon us. Things still seemed the same as I sat there, so I stood up and hurried back to town. I had to see Aunt El and Kat. I felt faith and confidence coursing through my bloodstream.

Aunt El and Kat were on the back porch when I arrived. I ran up the steps, anxious to share my news about the crystal. Before I could say anything, Kat grabbed my arm.

"Aunt El has some news for us," she said. I could tell she was bursting to tell. Aunt El looked tired, but her eyes no longer held the look of doom that had terrified me earlier. She smiled.

"Miss Tally has offered us the two vacant rooms. She has an extra sewing machine that belonged to her mother. She has offered it to me so that I can continue my sewing. She said she would wait for the rent until I could pay it if we would help out in the garden. Some of the merchants have offered clothing and personal items. It is wonderful, Sylvia. It is a true miracle!"

"I can buy the threads and material, whatever you need, Aunt El. I'll be paid tomorrow."

"Thank you, Sylvia," she said softly.

"Aunt El," I said, "I know it's a miracle, but it's also the crystal. I used it today. I found it in the fire and used it!"

Aunt El was silent. She seemed to be studying my face. Something seemed to flash into her eyes and then disappear.

Kat was wide eyed. She danced around us in excitement.

"It worked, it worked!" she said happily. "Plus you've used it! Is it mine now?"

I nodded and smiled. I felt sad inside to no longer be the owner, but it was only fair that it be given to Kat now.

Aunt El spoke quietly, "Let me have the crystal, Sylvia," she said.

She turned to Kat. "This is yours now, Kat, but I would like to keep it for you. Please." Kat looked confused but Aunt El seemed almost desperate in her quiet way to possess the crystal. "Okay," she said, reluctantly.

"Don't worry," Aunt El said softly. "When the time comes I will send the crystal to you. Now, perhaps we should look at the new clothes we've been so kindly offered!" Kat was instantly distracted and ran to freshen up for our shopping trip. I was excited, too, but an uneasy question brushed my thoughts. Why had Aunt El decided to keep the crystal for Kat?

Before I had a chance to explore that thought more deeply, Kat was back, babbling her enthusiasm, and we were off to shop.

Chapter Nine

The girls all arrived at once in the van Katie had borrowed from Billy Mac to use while her car was being repaired. Billy Mac was in the final stages of a repair job he had stretched out for three years. Katie didn't mind, though. As long as he provided random transportation, she was cheerfully accepting. Alba had arrived earlier. The aroma of some imaginary plant in the kitchen had convinced her that her father's spirit was surrounding her. She said it was his favorite plant. Everyone was in a good mood. Darrie was celebrating her first paycheck from Cut it Cute. Katie and Kat were planning a party. Kat did a lot of catering work on the side and Katie often helped out. Mandy was appearing as herself. I could tell by the frail way she brushed her hair back and slumped in the chair. Darrie was sticking close to her, hoping that Liz would wander in. Alba had cooked up a delicate key lime pie. Unfortunately, Kat was still ill-tempered over the banana bread incident, real or perceived, and brought her famous Mississippi mud pie. The mud pie was a hands-down winner on any occasion. Sadly, I would have to eat the key lime pie to save hard feelings. I knew the mud pie would stand its ground.

Darrie was anxious for advice. When she visited her boyfriend, Chuck, the previous Sunday, she had ran into Chuck's wife and five kids. The kids all were mirror images of Chuck. She tried to pick out the three he said did not belong to him. Darrie said his wife was a bitter woman with dry hair. She had stood ahead of Darrie in the visitors line outside the county jail where they waited their turn to approach the intercom and shout their name and the name of the inmate they wanted to visit. When Darrie heard the wife shout Chuck's name above the noise of the kids, she was so upset, she told us, she had to leave the line.

Before Darrie could finish her story, a small voice said, "I want my kitty."

"Here we go," Katie said, "that's the younger twin!"

"I had a little kitten," the voice continued. "My mama took out an insurance policy on it for fifty thousand dollars, then she let it sleep under the car hood. When she started her car, my kitty fell out. She jumped all around and then ran away."

"She's always making up stories about Mama that are not true," Katie said stoutly.

Suddenly Mandy stood up and slammed the table hard. "Harlot," a hard voice shouted, "you know nothing of the suffering this child has endured! I saw what Mama did!"

Katie cringed back in her chair. She whispered, "It's the preacher!"

Mandy leapt from her chair and begin pacing. She raised her long fingers and shouted venom and vengence.

"This house is full of bad spirits," Alba shouted, as she bolted out the door.

Katie seemed transfixed by the preacher. Of all the personalities, this was the one she hated most. She pressed her face into Kat's shoulder. Kat shook her off and stood up. She walked over and slapped the preacher in the face.

"I know what you did to Katie and Mandy in the basement," she said. "I know what you did to all of the little girls."

The preacher gave her a look of hatred. "You! You!" he sputtered, then dropped to the floor.

"I want my kitty," a small voice said in monotone.

Katie seemed to recover when she heard the small twin. She knelt by her sister and took her in her arms. In a few minutes Mandy stood up and looked around. "I don't feel well," she said.

We tried to act as though nothing had happened, but it was hopeless. The girls were too upset, and I felt tired inside. I looked at the girls and at myself and saw damages. I wondered if anyone ever made it through life without them. Beautiful merchandise destroyed by rough hands. Trust betrayed.

Chapter Ten

Mrs. Crank had ordered a huge piece of light lavender silk. I could barely carry it into her room. We spent the morning arranging it. We pushed her bed up under her tiny window. Next we draped the window, pinning it at the top and around the wall. We pulled the front piece out over the bed and pinned it, too.

"Does it look sultry," she asked?

"A sultan may appear at any moment," I said. She laughed. She had spent the week reading *The Geisha Girl's Story of Sex*, and the bedroom description inspired her to redecorate. She threw some colored throw pillows on the bed. Even the lamp was covered by a purple scarf. She loved to create romantic illusions.

"Soft lights are good for the soul," she said, "particularly after forty." I agreed. By the time we were content with the new look, it was time for lunch. We decided to eat at the drop leaf table outside, tucked neatly into the white gazebo, and surrounded by bright flowers. We had tuna salad and rolls, provided by the home, and goat cheese and wine, provided by the local deli and wine shop. Mrs. Crank wanted to hear about the latest Friday night gathering. I told her everything that had taken place. She nodded and listened carefully. I thought she would ask about the personalities, but instead she lingered on Alba. She thought her outburst and the bolt from the house was very odd, but she urged me to, "Just try to be understanding."

Mrs. Crank was also interested in the Mississippi mud pie dessert and I was sorry that I had not thought to bring her a piece. She asked if I'd bring flowers the next day. She wanted pink roses to keep in her room. No problem.

When I arrived home, Kat was sleeping in my bed. I crawled in beside of her and fell asleep.

Chapter Eleven

On Monday morning, Alba dropped by with an apology for calling the house a den of bad spirits and running away. She said that Mandy's spirit had overwhelmed her.

She didn't know if she could handle another Friday night with Mandy. I told her not to worry, that Mandy was leaving to live with her mother in Florida. Alba brightened up considerably at the news. She had another problem, however, and confessed it was driving her nuts. Her house had to be fumigated in a couple of weeks and she couldn't afford a motel. She needed a place to stay for a few days.

"Usually," I said, "when the exterminator comes, we just leave for the day. It's perfectly safe to return by evening." In other words, please, God, no, do not ask to stay here.

"Oh, I know," Alba said, "but it's not the usual exterminating job. I'm having the house tented, you know, covered with a huge tent. It takes three days."

"Why," I asked. "That's a little extreme, isn't it? I mean, your house is spotless. The exterminating is just a precaution."

"Oh, no, I don't have bugs," she said, "It's the ghost smells and the lost spirits."

I wanted to be understanding, and I knew that I would be, but still, just once in my life, I would so love to have a normal friend. Some innocent, gentle, chatty soul who wanted nothing more than an occasional coffee and movie date. I know it would be lovely. I just know it.

"Alba," I said, "how much does it cost to have lost spirits and the smell of ghosts removed?"

"Well, I wrestled a really good deal out of him. Twelve hundred dollars! A flat rate." She beamed at her own brilliance and ability to cut a deal. Hmm, I thought, can't afford a motel, but able to spend a fortune on insanity.

"I could stay with you. It would be so much fun!" She was very happy with the idea. I smiled. This was not the first time that Ms. Manners had slapped her hypocritical hand on my shoulder. I'm not a virgin to the horrible consequences that can sometimes appear hand in hand with politeness.

"Yes, wonderful," I said, "but as fun as that would be, I have a simpler solution."

"What," she asked.

"A séance. It wouldn't cost you a thing. The girls would be happy to help, and I'm sure between the five of us we could eliminate any lingering, loitering ghosts."

"I don't know," she said, pondering the idea. I held my breath; even my heart stopped a moment to listen.

"You know, that's not a bad idea."

Thank God, I thought to myself, breathing again.

"Do you think the girls would really help? I have a bar in the kitchen, or we could use that old ping pong table in the basement. Yes, I think it would work. I feel like we can do it."

"I know we can do it," I said emphatically, "I feel it in my heart." Which was beating happily once more.

"But I don't want Mandy there. And we will need to do it this Friday," she said. "We can have coffee afterwards."

"I said five, didn't I? It will be fine," I said. I felt as though I had left the beach one day before the hurricane of the decade hit. Now all I had to do was sell the girls on the idea. Darrie was always willing to help anyone. Kat would be bitter, but loyal. Katie had a dread and fear of the dark, but was reluctant to be left out of any event that might prove interesting.

"I have to go to the grocery store, Alba," I said. "We'll talk more about this later. Please try not to worry."

"All right," she said. "I'm going home, getting online and ordering some herbs. You know, one must have the right conditions for a séance."

I grabbed my pocketbook and keys and followed her out. I forgot my grocery list, but didn't want to go back. I'd just have to count on my memory.

The store was practically deserted, just the way I liked it. I took my time and started at the organic aisle. I love to check out the cheeses and breads. The vegetables were lovely; the chicken hand fed and pampered into its package. I love the organic aisle passionately. I do not, however, ever have the money to shop there. That gentle, grain raised cow obviously ate its weight in gold. Nothing in the aisle was available to a normal budget. I had tried the small jar of peanut butter once. It cost five dollars, but was filled with the richness of the natural earth. Man had not dallied with the nuts. I had eaten it the moment I arrived home. It was delicious, and the milk, which was tampered with by man, was also good. I was pleased with my purchase until the next day when I tried to scoop it from the jar. First I had to plunge through a topping of healthy oil that faked me into believing moistness awaited. Then I had to try and stir the whole mess into the oil, seeking consistent smoothness.

Unfortunately, the peanut butter felt at home where it lay in a solid, rock hard lump. I still had my own teeth, but I didn't want to risk anything. Eventually, I left it alone, uneasy that I had paid five dollars for one peanut butter sandwich, but proud that my body had, for once, actually entertained organic food. As I followed my usual beaten path around the store, I remembered most of the items from my list. I felt confident of my purchases, except maybe the yogurt. I knew it held health benefits, so I grabbed two righteous strawberry cups, but possibly undid all my good by adding a chocolate mousse yogurt that was actually edible.

There was a woman in front of me at checkout with cheese, crackers, and two bottles of wine. She was happily telling the cashier about a party that night. She was giddy with excitement and anxious to share. The cashier was a sullen, skinny girl with issues. One of them was conversational customers.

"Excuse me," she said to the woman, "I have to call the manager." The woman looked puzzled. The manager arrived at a crawl.

"What is the problem," he asked, possibly not happy at leaving the break room.

"This woman is drunk," the cashier said.

The woman was astonished. If the cashier disliked happy campers, she no longer had to worry. The woman was now a cold, enraged version of her former self.

"I am not drunk," she said. "Are you insane?"

The manager looked at the contents on the counter.

"Ma'am," he said, "we can't sell you that alcohol. You are too intoxicated."

"I am not drunk," the woman said loudly.

"I am afraid we will have to ask you to leave," he said, "You're creating a public scene.

You are drunk and disorderly and we must ask you to leave the premises!"

The woman left in humiliation. I was really astonished by the exchange. I put my order on the counter. The girl rang it up with a small smile on her lips.

I paid with a check and wrote slow. I could tell she was the type that would hate it. She slapped the check in the drawer without looking at it. We completed the transaction at last. She failed to say thank you.

"That woman was not drunk," I said, my groceries safely in the buggy. "If you dislike your job, find another one."

"Are you drunk, too?" she asked with a warning smirk.

"Nope," I said. "Manager!"

The manager shuffled back over.

"I wrote my check for five dollars over, as the sign clearly states that it is permissible, but this young woman has closed the drawer and failed to deliver my money."

He gave the cashier a cold look and opened the register himself.

"I am very sorry ma'am," he said. "I will see that it doesn't happen again."

Chapter Twelve

On Wednesday I visited my therapist for our bi-weekly evaluation of my inability to maintain normal relationships with men. I had maintained a relationship with the doctor for fifteen years, but he claimed that didn't count. He wanted me to establish relationships with good men. Since he was the only good man I knew at the moment, I tried to keep our appointments. I thought this was a good point, but he asked that I not hide my emotions behind humor. He was a kind, intelligent, caring man. I wanted very badly to impress him with my progress, but each session was a litany of failure.

"What about the girls," I asked. "I've maintained a relationship with them for years!"

He raised his brows. "We won't go into that mish-mash of disorders," he said, "focus on the issue at hand."

I also had a problem with alcohol. Not that I drank, but that I have a magnetic energy field that attracts alcoholics like a neon sign. I had endured a number of failed relationships. I liked alcoholics. They were the only men I knew that liked to laugh and dance and sing. At first, anyway. After a few months with me, depression invariably set in. Then the laughter stopped and the brooding stepped right in. All my relationships started with an interesting, fun guy, and ended with a bitter broth of blame and accusations. I usually ended the relationship, like a bad mother, by giving them symbolic candy and claiming I would be right back.

Today Doc looked worried. I told him he looked depressed and awkwardly asked if he wanted to talk about it.

He laughed and said no. I didn't say anything else in case he started the "hiding behind humor" thing again.

"So, how was your week?" he asked.

I have bad dreams and unfounded fears. Sometimes the fears are for loved ones and sometimes for myself. The doctor says that I have an avoidance personality disorder. It affects both my social and interpersonal relationships. It isn't that I don't want relationships with others, but that I avoid them out of fear. He says the disorder is marked by social withdrawal, shyness, mistrustfulness, and emotional distance. I listen politely. He did, after all, study such things for years, and I wish to show the proper amount of respect. He believes that I assumed too much responsibility too young. He claims that even when I repeat events to him, it's as though I'm an unemotional observer. I feel badly about it. I can only tell him—or anyone—events as they happened. But I have to admit to often breezing past the painful, emotional aspects of a situation. It's how I survive. I told him all the latest happenings while he sat quietly, nodding. When I finished, he asked to hear more about the minister. Why had Mandy used the minister to intimidate Katie?

"I don't know," I said. "Maybe she feels guilty."

"Why does she feel guilty? What happened?"

"Well," I said, "it's an ugly story." I only know what Katie told me a long time ago. Their mother was a very odd woman, their father a sheep-like man who simply followed orders. The mother had lots of rules for bringing up children. She was very religious, too. Katie and Mandy were the youngest and the last two at home. School dismissed at four o'clock in the evening. Mama made them do homework, eat supper, and take a bath each evening, rushing them through these tasks so that they would be in bed by six. It was difficult to meet her deadline, but they managed to do so in order to avoid her stick. Mama had a stick of green wood, just flexible enough for a good swing. She also made them attend church on Sunday morning and Sunday afternoon. Mama adored the minister, Reverend Shell. When he asked if the girls could clean his church on Saturday afternoons, Mama was pleased to send them. They were never allowed to do anything on Saturdays, anyway, so they liked the arrangement. It at least got them out of the house. Katie was nine, Mandy was seven.

The first Saturday Reverend Shell watched as they cleaned. He joked with them a great deal and complimented them on each job as they completed it. He fixed grape Kool-Aid and brought it to them himself. He was really nice, they told each other, and they were gleeful that their Mama was pleased, as well. She served them a nice supper when they arrived home. She gave them extra dessert.

She bragged about them on the phone to her own mother. The next Saturday, Katie and Mandy were happy to hurry off to the church. Reverend Shell gave Mandy a broom and told her to sweep the front steps. He asked Katie to clean the small hymnal room in the back. Sometimes Reverend Shell slept there on Saturdays if he stayed too late writing his sermon. Katie started to wipe down the shelves. Rev. Shell told her he had to rest and he removed all his clothing. Katie was surprised, but only because he wasn't wearing long johns. Her father always wore them, even in the summer.

When Rev. Shell grabbed her from behind, she thought she was being punished. She was always being punished by Mama. When he raped her, she did not even scream. The pain was terrible, but she was too ashamed to cry in front of Rev. Shell. After it was over, he cleaned her up and sent her outside to sweep. He took Mandy into the room and told Katie to stay on the porch. When Mandy began screaming inside the church, Katie kept sweeping. She wanted to help Mandy. She wanted to be bigger than Rev. Shell and help Mandy, but she was afraid. When Rev. Shell came outside, he was holding a handful of money. He told Katie to go for her Mama and to tell her Mandy was not feeling well. He sent the money to Mama. Katie was happy to go home, even though Mama made her go right to bed. This time, Katie did not care.

When Mama returned, she was carrying Mandy. She gave Mandy a bath. Mandy missed school for a week. After that, Mama made Katie clean the church alone. Katie cleaned the church each Saturday for the next few years. The abuse did not end until she was caught kissing a boy on her front porch. Then Mama told her to leave. She said Katie was no good. When I finished the story, Doc was silent.

"When Mandy goes home to Mama, how long do you think she will stay?"

"A long time," I said. Then I noticed my time was up.

Chapter Thirteen

I waited until Friday morning to mention the séance to Kat. She was not thrilled with the idea.

"Yeah, right!" she said. "I'm going to sit in a whacko's basement at a ping pong table holding hands and smelling for ghosts."

"Please ,Kat," I begged, "I promise to buy you a new pair of jeans this weekend if you go along with this."

Katie is kind of scared of this kind of thing, the dark, the ghosts— Alba by candlelight. She sighed. "Any jeans I choose?"

"Yes, I won't even hover over the price tag."

"Okay," she said, "We'll be there, but I'm not bringing any food. I just want to get in and get out."

"That's fair," I said. "Thanks, Kat."

I was busy paying bills most of the day. Alba called and asked if everyone had agreed to the séance, and I reassured her that we would all be there.

The girls arrived early and we all walked over to Alba's. She answered the door wearing a long purple dress and bandana. I could just about feel Kat rolling her eyes behind me. Alba's house has the same layout as mine, but the similarity ends there. My house is an assortment of odd pieces, none of them worth very much. There was really no color scheme. My basic intent was simplicity and cleanliness. Everything in Alba's house matched in a rush of mauve and burgundy. She had stenciled delicate flowers in a beautiful border around the top of the walls. End tables, each holding a rose-colored lamp, stood at each end of the sofa. The sofa was woven with roses. A white rug lay on the floor. The floors were so clean that if a roach ever wandered through by mistake, he'd probably commit suicide.

Alba led us downstairs to the ping pong room. She had draped the table with a red checked cloth, and arranged aluminum folding chairs, where we all took a seat.

The aroma of incense flowed through the air. There were no windows and the air was stuffy and hot. She was the only one standing. She reached into the huge pockets of her dress and pulled out some herbs that she sprinkled freely in a circle around the table.

"This creates a ring of protection," she said. "The spirits cannot pass through to hinder us in the ceremony."

Alba lit an oil lamp and placed it in the center of the table. She said the good spirits would be drawn to the flame. They would love the light, but the bad spirits would linger in the darkness until she sent them to hell. It all sounded very dramatic. Katie was pressed so closely to Kat that it appeared that they were sitting in the same chair. Darrie was glancing around the room. She was very quiet. I just wished that Alba would get on with the séance.

Suddenly she hit the switch and the room darkened. The only source of a light was the oil lamp. It flickered on the faces around me, creating an eerie movement of shadows. Alba asked us to all hold hands. She sat at the head of the table. She grasped my hand on one side and Katie's on the other. Kat was beside Katie and Darrie was next to me. Darrie's hand was warm and sweaty. I felt as though I was suffocating in the heat. Alba said she had written a request that she would be speaking aloud. She would be asking the ghosts to come forward voluntarily. Then she would request that they leave and never return. It all sounded simple enough. Alba began speaking. We listened for any replies that might be seduced into the open.

"Oh, Great Spirit God, Spirit of my father, Spirit of Nature and Man, send forth the spirits that haunt this house with their foul odors and whispered laughter in the middle of the night when I am trying to sleep."

It seemed very direct and accusatory to me. Aunt El always said you could lure more flies with honey than vinegar. Alba may have heard my thoughts because she switched lanes suddenly in her appeal.

"Oh, Dear Ghosts, Lost Souls and Pitiful Spirits, come forth that ye might receive comfort and healing at the hands of Alba, your friend, your haunted and housemate." Alba stopped speaking and it grew very quiet. Everyone seemed to hold their breath. It was so black in the shadows. The lamp threw little light over the table. It was hard to make out each face; only the hands entwined around the table could be seen clearly. The spirits were probably confused, one minute accused of foul odors and the next being cuddled as dear souls. Either way, Alba's chant was lengthy and repetitive, and my foot had fallen asleep. Finally, she stopped to wait for a response. I figured the ghosts might have left the house out of boredom.

Suddenly a rank smell filled the air. We all gagged, some of us indelicately, then jerked our hands free to cover our mouths for some full blown retching sounds at the horrible smell of dirt, feces, and something hard to identify but impossible to ignore. Alba was the only one not reacting similarly. She was lifting her arms in excitement and screaming for the ghosts to continue to come forth. She planned to get them out where she could rid of all of them at once. Katie moved her hands from over her nose to over her ears. She kept her eyes shut. Kat had one hand over her nose, and a sharp eye on Alba. Darrie had her face hidden in my shoulder. She had reverted to the childhood theory that what you can't see, can't see you. We heard a sound that could have been laughter, like a child gurgling, or maybe a strangled giggle. The smell was growing stronger by the minute. I wished Alba would stop invoking spirits long enough for me to catch my breath.

Kat came around the table and leaned over to whisper, "Where the heck is the light switch?" None of the other girls had ever visited Alba. I stood up and turned on the light. Alba whirled around, stunned and furious. She was right in the midst of a long invoking moment. She was also right in the middle of a stream of mud and feces. It was dribbling from a crack in the wall and dripping slowly to the cement floor.

"Hey," Kat said, "it looks like your sewer needs to be pumped."

Alba wasn't one to give ground without a fight. "It's the ghosts," she insisted. "They have the ability to shift shapes into anything they choose."

"Oh, brother!" Kat said. "You mean you think you have ghosts that shift into—"

"Kat," I said, before she could finish her sentence, "I think we should all go upstairs. It can't be very healthy to breathe this stuff."

"That's true," Darrie said. "It could be full of poisonous gasses"

Alba was the last one up the stairs. She stomped up in a fury of disappointment and humiliation. All her ghosts down the drain, so to speak.

"Don't worry, Alba," I said. "I can give you the name of the guy that comes out when my sewer backs up. He's very reasonable. He charges me four hundred dollars, but he does a great job and guarantees his work."

She was still tight-lipped and upset, cheated out of the séance she had worked so hard to make a success. Not only that, her sense of smell had betrayed her, publicly.

"What kind of woman can't decipher between a ghost and a sewer," she said bitterly.

Even Kat felt sorry for her. I could tell when she commented on the stenciling. She said it took a great deal of skill and attention to detail to stencil. I often thought that Alba's house had the sterile look of someone living out of a suitcase, always poised to disappear to some distant place. Nothing we said worked to improve her mood, so we finally thanked her and headed back to my kitchen. Alba said she was going to bed. She said she felt a migraine climbing up behind her eyes like thunder. Still, at least she had saved a bit of money. It cost a lot less to pump a sewer than to tent the house.

Chapter Fourteen

I was having trouble sleeping. Not an uncommon thing, but, perhaps because it eluded me so often, I had a passion for sleep. I had rituals that I rendered unto sleep, as though serving a goddess. White noise was key to the equation. I had a fan in the bedroom that rivaled a freight train. I scented the sheets with sunflower spray, and kept an electric blanket on low for warmth. Surely sleep would be enticed.

Tonight I was tossing because of the Alabama Crystal. The first night I'd received it, I had secured it in the bottom of my cedar hope chest. I knew that it was to be passed to Kat. I knew that Kat would be shocked, but thrilled to finally have it as her own. The problem that was bothering me was the fact that the crystal had been lost for so long. How had it reappeared so many years later? Sometimes the crystal seemed somewhat of a curse; it granted one thing and took away another. It was both a curse and a blessing. I tried to dismiss such a thought, but it persisted uneasily on my mind. The address appeared to be in Aunt El's handwriting. The letter was definitely postmarked Wayward, Georgia. It was a mystery. It was unnerving to see Aunt El's handwriting. She had been dead a long time.

Since I could not sleep anyway, I closed my eyes and let my mind drift back to Wayward.

Soon, I found myself back at Miss Tally's bed and breakfast. Miss Tally was a woman of her word. She let us have the two rooms and waited like an angel for the money. The merchants came through with clothing and I used my small paycheck for sewing supplies. Aunt El resumed her sewing business. Since we were living in town, the work doubled, and soon Kat was asking to help out. I had never mastered the needle, but Kat had inherited the neat, precise stitches Aunt El was known for. Aunt El gave Kat spending money for helping out. Aunt El loved it in town, and never mentioned the old home place or the fire that destroyed it. She sold the land to Mr. Jacobs and deposited the money in the bank in a trust fund for Kat and me. It was a nice sum of money. Aunt El did not have to use it at all since her business had improved so much in town. As soon as Kat graduated, she planned to send both of us off to college. Kat and I loved to sprawl out and research schools. We lay across the bed, our feet in the air, our heads full of dreams. Everything had changed in our lives, but for the better. I asked Aunt El about the crystal, but she assured me that it was in a safe place and, when the time was right, it would be there for Kat. I assumed she had placed it in the bank in her security box. Kat never mentioned it at all. She was busy with her best friend, Katie, and with the choir auditions at church. Kat had a beautiful voice and was thrilled that the church had invited her to sing. She practiced constantly and her singing became a wonderful background for our new home.

Chapter Fifteen

I woke up tired. Mrs. Crank took note of it instantly and suggested we have tea outside. We took her beautiful tea set outside and placed it on the picnic table provided for visitors. Mrs. Crank insisted I lay out the entire set in case someone dropped by. I made the tea in the kitchen and took it outside.

The tea set looked lovely in the sunlight that filtered through the trees. Her husband brought it from China, and she valued it highly. The set was in a small burgundy and green box. The cups looked like small thimbles. On the outside of the box, it said, "Jing Pin Zi Sha Zhen Cang Xi Lie."

"I do not speak Chinese," Mrs. Crank said. "I assume that is the name of the set."

"Maybe it says 'Made in China,'" I suggested.

Mrs. Crank smiled. "Perhaps so."

The china was a lovely green shade, and the cups had small flowers in the bottom. I loved the delicate, otherworldly feel of having tea with Mrs. Crank. She was in her flowing white linen pants and shirt today. Her hair was pinned in an upswept style, and her eyes were large and lively. We were relaxed and happy, offering tea to other residents as they drifted by. I also felt sleepy, and wished I could pocket it for tonight and take it like a pill at bedtime.

"How was the séance," Mrs. Crank asked, taking a sip from her dainty cup.

"Well," I said, "it was successful in clearing up the mystery of the odors that have invaded Alba's house, but the only thing we conjured up appears to be lots of old waste."

I told her about the ping pong table and the sewer and the ritual that brought them together. She laughed a great deal. People fascinated her, and she had a real interest in Alba. I was pleased to see she was sympathetic to Alba and seemed to wish her well.

"She is nothing like her mother, really," Mrs. Crank said.

"You knew Alba's mother?" I said, astonished.

"Yes, dear," Mrs. Crank said. "We were great friends until the day she died. One of my first intentions in heaven will be to look her up."

Mrs. Crank took my hand. She only did this when she wanted me to listen very closely.

"Sylvia, it is important to me that you are good to Alba. Remember, there is always a lot more to people than we can see on the surface. At the moment, Alba is wearing a façade. I hope you will remain kind when the façade finally cracks." Of course, I plunged into a half dozen questions, but Mrs. Crank only smiled. Giving up on garnering any more information, I finally called it a day and hugged her goodbye. I decided to visit Cut It Cute on Wednesday for a shampoo and trim. I also had an appointment with Doc, who liked to see me implement actions of self-improvement. My experience with hair usually involved shampoo in the shower, a quick stint with the blow dryer, and then pinning the whole show up haphazardly. I arrived when everyone was having lunch, so there was no mad rush to wait on me.

Darrie spied me and dashed over. She was enjoying only a diet drink for lunch, so her hands were ready to spring into action. She dropped the chair back and went to work, bending over me in a fury of scrubbing. While I was lying defenseless, staring up at her cleavage and avoiding the bounce, she suggested that I have my brows done. I declined quickly. Most people could have their brows done and it would enlarge their eyes in an appealing way. I had tried a couple of times before and it was always the same: a sharp startled look, as though I had been jolted by electricity. I explained this to Darrie in my thanks-but-no-thanks statement.

"Ah," she said, "you have just not encountered the right person for the job. I promise not to take off very much."

Every woman knows that this promise is in the code that students memorize in beauty school. They know, and yet, while captured in the fumes of hairspray, hair gel, perm formulas, and dye, they drift into a sort of trance. It is a lovely trance where perfection and beauty settles on them in their cozy laid back chair and whispers, "Yes, yes, this time you will be beautiful". So it was with my misgivings and me, and it was not until Darrie had completed her work, and I stood to pay that reality came sharply into focus, in the mirror behind the register. My original intentions glared back at me indignantly. On the way to Doc's office I kept looking in the rearview mirror. Each time a look of startled surprise met me. I knew it would stay there for several months, until my brow hair once more formed a normal, placid mien.

Doc tried not to do a double take at the frightened face before him.

"I am trying to improve myself," I explained, perhaps a bit defensively.

"Yes, yes, I can see that," he said. "Very good! You look lovely."

He actually said this with a straight face. He is a kind, polite man. I felt warmly toward him. I did not, however, wish to endanger his soul with the burden of white lies, so I changed the subject. We discussed some of my issues with men, my distaste of confrontation, and how to set boundaries. I forgot to mention that I am terrible at setting boundaries. Doc mentions it often. Then I felt my hands and feet growing cold. Since it was warm in his office, I realized it was panic. I remained calm, smiled politely and said I should be going. I even paused at the desk to make a payment. My casual walk to the car held no clue of fear or upset. My face might be lacking in expression, but my body danced with relief. I cannot bear to be inside during a panic attack. I am certain that Doc would have been of great assistance to me, but I hate to be vulnerable. I also have a fear that people will dislike me. As the rock and roll song says, there was a whole lot of shaking going on.

I opened all the windows in the car. Usually a devoted fan of air conditioning, the thought of closed windows sickened me. Once I was moving up the street, I turned the radio up loud enough to rock the car. I pretended to search through my purse at red lights. A middle-aged woman in a sedate sedan shaking with music sometimes creates gawking situations. I took half a Xanax; my hands were shaking so it took a moment to bite it precisely in half. Now I also appeared to be a druggie! But my large, dark sunglasses made me feel invisible. I was such at pro at panic now that I drove directly to the hospital and sat outside. The doctors and nurses there knew me very well. Believe me when I say that doctors and nurses dislike panic attacks. They have really sick people to deal with. They have ambulances parked outside to prove it. I have nothing to prove that I am sick. I cannot even prove it to myself. So I sit there. I put the seat back and listen to music and sing. Singing distracts panic attacks. The two have nothing in common. One dallies with worries, the other with lyrics. They do not even like to be in the same car together. Eventually the panic moves on.

I wait a while longer, admiring the parking lot. I notice that I have failed to park between the lines correctly. I start the car, roll up all the windows but the driver's side, and cautiously rejoin the masses of faithfully unafraid people heading home. I arrive home in time to see a man in a white uniform giving a slip of paper to Alba. I assume it's an estimate, since there's a Sewer Rooter van. Alba must have connections to have him come out so quickly. I wonder about his white uniform. Why would they possibly wear white? Was it a sign of how sterile and clean things could be? Were they not afraid of stains? I imagined wives everywhere whining, "Do you have to wear white?" Or maybe it was just me. I'm always a little delirious with relief when a panic attack subsides. I am also very tired and drained. It is as though I've just won a war where a thousand huge emotions are charging the barricades and I fought them off alone. Of course, the half of Xanax helped tremendously. It also made me very sleepy. I went in and dropped lengthways on the couch. I was so pleased when sleep slid in beside me.

Chapter Sixteen

Katie, of course, grew up in Wayward, the same as Kat and I. Her father was a traveling salesman and rarely seen in town. Mother was a housewife. According to Katie, she was also terribly strict. Kat disliked her because Katie was never allowed to come outside after school. Once Katie was caught by her mother in a compromising position with a boy, she packed her small bag of clothes and put her outside. I'm not sure if she intended to let her back in or not, but Katie, as headstrong as she was beautiful, set out on her own. She hitchhiked up north and stayed for four years. She had a miscarriage, married, had another baby, and returned home. She and her husband rented a house in town, and Katie found a job at the laundry. Her husband disappeared a week later. A month later, his mother appeared and asked for the baby boy. Katie loved the baby, but knew she could not support them both. Tearfully, but determined to do the best for her son, she allowed him to go. Kat begged to stay over at Katie's a couple nights a week. Katie was always welcome at our place, and was a frequent guest, as she loved Miss Tally's cooking, which was, admittedly, several notches up from her own.

When Katie's mother found out she was in town, she asked everyone to give her a cold shoulder. This worked at her church, but our church and most of the rest of the town's folks loved Katie. She was outgoing and kind to everyone, always willing to help anyone who asked. Aunt El and Miss Tally had developed an excellent friendship. They were both nurturing, selfless women with a great love for children. Our lives were falling in place so well. It was a happy time, filled with laughter. I was still working part time and waiting for Kat to finish her last month of school. In two weeks she would graduate. Aunt El brought catalogs home for Kat to look through. She told her to find something that she really wanted. One Saturday, we were looking through the catalogs while Aunt El and Miss Tally were in town finding flowers for Mother's Day at the church. The youngest and oldest mother at church on Mother's Day would receive flowers. The mother with the most children would also. We took the catalogs to the front porch and began pinning cutouts of possible gift choices onto the porch posts. We were surprised to hear the crunch of gravel as the Sheriff made his way up the path to the porch.

When he reached us, he took his hat off, wiped his brow and then his eyes. He looked tired and sad as he searched our faces.

"I have some bad news, girls," he said. Kat and I both looked blankly at him. "It is hard to say this, but Miss Tally and your Aunt El have been in a bad accident." He said that a truck carrying a load of cattle had lost its brakes and veered into the floral shop where Miss Tally and Aunt El were standing. They had just stepped outside, each with an armful of flowers. He said they never saw what hit them.

"What do you mean," Kat asked.

"I mean they were killed instantly. I am terribly sorry to have to deliver this kind of news, and I want you to know I'm here if either of you girls need anything. I'd like for you to ride with me over to the funeral home."

Kat and I stared at the Sheriff in amazement. He was calm and gentle, and drew us to him, one under each arm, as we sobbed in horror. It was a sunny day. Could someone we loved die on such a beautiful day? Could anyone? Later it begin to rain, the way it does in the south when the day has been too hot and earth and sky grow irritable and seem to argue. The Sheriff took us to the funeral home and stood by as we made arrangements. The director there guided us through the process. He had Aunt El's purse. I took out her checkbook and handed him a check. He ushered us back to the Sheriff, who took us home, where Kat and I sat in shock.

Women from the church appeared, bringing food and comfort. They were very kind and stood by us throughout the wake and burial. We had chosen a beautiful lavender casket. It was Aunt El's favorite color. From the profusion of blossoms, it appeared that everyone in town had sent flowers. We listened to the words of the minister, but in our hearts we heard the voice of Aunt El. Her love and devotion had been the solid support beam of our lives. A brother of Miss Tally had been notified. He was out the country but would be arriving in a week.

Finally it was all over. Aunt El lay in the gated green cemetery. Mounds of the beautiful flowers she loved covered her grave, most of them purple irises and, her personal favorite, lilacs. Eventually, we had to turn and walk away. We declined all offers of rides and walked hand in hand through the humidity. Our clothes clung to our bodies as we clung to each other. I could see the same dawning in Kat's eyes that I knew shone from my own. I shivered in the heat. We were orphans.

Chapter Seventeen

Katie took Mandy to Florida in one of Billy Mac's small cars. They had little money and needed something to drive that was easy on gas. Alba had her sewer pumped and stopped complaining of bad odors. It was just the four of us for the Friday night coffee. Kat walked in and lay some fudge brownies on the table.

"You look surprised to see me," she said, then laughed. She was referring to my pencil brow.

"I see the magic of the salon sang you once more into the lullaby of belief." I rolled my eyes. I would have raised my eyebrows significantly, but they were already stenciled so high there was no need. Darrie told me to ignore Kat, that I looked classy and alert. Then she asked about Katie and Mandy. Why had Mandy left so suddenly?

"I'm not sure," Kat said. "I think it was the night we all went out to sing. Mandy called her mother to ask if she would send money. Her mother said she had money but would not send it. She promised her a car and some cash, but only if she'd come home. Katie plans to spend the night and start back the next day. Her mother never allows her to stay long."

"What about her dad?" Darrie said. "He seems nice."

"He is," Kat agreed, "but totally controlled by his wife. She comes from a long line of moneyed misers and tells her hubby when to take a breath and how deep. Katie is his secret favorite. She looks just like him. Unlike him, she's impossible to control, so Mama ignores her."

"That's sad," Darrie said. "My new guy, Charles, is great. He is so careful to never be controlling. I work as late as I need to and he never says a word! I pay the bills and pick out the groceries. Of course, I insist he make a list of some of his favorites. I know now what they are, but at first I kept making mistakes."

"Does he have a job yet?" Kat asked bluntly.

"No, but he stays online all day filling out applications. He's put his whole heart into it. The problem is he can't find a job that pays what he's used to making. He says he will settle for less if that's what I want, but I told him to keep looking. I want him to know I have faith in him."

"What about his kids?" Alba said, "Doesn't he want them to have faith in him?"

"Of course he does," Darrie said indignantly, "but I've told you how the situation is. He's just not sure they are really his kids. Plus his wife gets all kinds of help from the state—food stamps, Medicaid, and housing! He doesn't want to mess that up for her. She has a boyfriend, too. He said he hated to support a grown man with money meant for his kids."

"If she has a new boyfriend, why was she at the jail visiting him," Kat asked. Darrie suddenly looked like a deer caught in headlights. Darrie's kind of love was true, but it came with a big blindfold. I felt sorry for her. I knew how it was to love someone more than you loved yourself.

"Hey, Alba," I said, "they're having a big party at the home, do you think we could borrow your ping pong table? Mrs. Crank asked me to invite you. She said she'd pay you to make a pineapple upside down cake."

Alba preened proudly, cutting her eyes toward Kat for a flicker of a second.

"I will be happy to loan them the table. Tell Mrs. Crank that I would not dream of charging her. I enjoy donating for a good cause."

"Well, it is a good cause," I said. "Mrs. Crank wants to liven up the place. She has requested a band. She also received permission to turn the dining room into a dance floor. It was no small feat to get that approved."

We discussed the party for a while. Everyone loved Mrs. Crank's refusal to sit still in a rocking chair. The evening ended quietly. Kat said she had to cater the Appalachian Winers the next day, and left to complete her cooking. Alba was the last to leave. She wanted more details about Mrs. Crank and the pineapple upside down cake. I told her that Mrs. Crank bragged outrageously to the nurses about her cooking. The lemon cake at Christmas had barely survived the rush when it was placed on the table. Alba was wonderful with donations. She loved appreciation. I watched her walk back to her house. She looked small in the glare of her porch light. I had never known Alba to date, although every couple of months she made trips to Atlanta to shop. Sometimes she went sight-seeing out west, as she had a passion for the mountains there. She loved to collect herbs and to work with homemade medicines. She felt that doctors, as a rule, prescribed far too much medication. The body was made for more natural ingredients, she would say firmly. It was a relief to me to have Alba next door. She often commented that she felt safer with my presence. The feeling was mutual. She was capable of some outrageous thinking, but, then, we all were.

Watching her enter her house, I prayed that she would have a good night. I repeated the same prayer for myself.

Chapter Eighteen

I sat on the Aunt El's bed going through her things. The brother would be arriving the next morning. The past few days had been unbearable. We had never been separated. It was always the three of us. The silence in the house was unfamiliar and cold. The emptiness of a beloved human being and the huge void left was too difficult to express. Each piece of clothing, each toiletry, the feather pillow she hugged up to at night, all seemed to be waiting. I longed to wait with them. Ridding the room of her things seemed to be a disloyalty, a lack of faith in her return. Where had the essence that was hers alone gone away to? It was impossible for Kat to help me. I had taken one look at her sleepless stare of grief and despair and surrendered any thought of her company in my task. All I can say of that time is that some grief is too strong to take at once, and must be cut into small doses.

After I emptied the room, I remembered the Alabama Crystal. It was not in any of the things I had packed. I made a note in my head to look for it in the strong box at the bank. Kat and I were closing out the balance. I wasn't sure yet how much it was. I only knew that the money was our future, and that we would have to be very careful.

Aunt El's room was empty. Kat and I had all our possessions waiting at the door for a cab. It was due to pick us up at five. I decided to walk down to the bank. The manager was very kind. I signed the withdrawal papers for the cash and produced the key for the strong box. He escorted me to the box. I found an old deed, a pearl necklace, and a couple of savings bonds. I did not see the Alabama Crystal. My heart sank. This was the last place it could be and I was stunned that it was missing. I asked the manager if Aunt El had another box. He said no. I could not understand why the crystal was missing, but I couldn't think of anyplace else to search for it. I took the contents of the box and picked up a thousand in cash and the balance check from the manager. Everything was signed and settled. I did not look at the check until I was outside. My heart beat swiftly and I felt a great weight lifting inside. The check was for one hundred and fifty thousand dollars. I was stunned. I hurried home to show Kat. I knew the money would help make her less afraid of the future. When I returned home, Kat was sitting on the porch steps biting her fingernails. The house was empty of our possessions. It was no longer a home, merely a house. Everything we owned was inside the three suitcases sitting neatly by Kat's side.

"Where are we going," Kat asked.

"Any place you like!" I said, trying to sound upbeat and enthusiastic. I produced the check with a flourish and Kat's eyes widened. "That's a lot of money."

"Yes," I said. "We should be able to buy a house and pay for college. Do you have any idea where you'd like to go?"

We had no solid plan of action formed. It was an odd feeling. We could decide our own destiny and fly out into it. Having been directed and protected all of our lives, it was frightening, yet exciting, to be making choices.

"I do have an idea, Sylvia, and I have something I want to tell you. Katie and I have been talking this past week. She has a friend in Roanoke, Virginia. Her friend is named Lacy Stuart. She is in a university there. Katie wants to go there, but she also wants to be with us. I think I'd like it there, too. Would it be okay with you if we went there and for Katie to come with us? She said that Lacy has her own apartment. She lives off campus and loves to have people stay in the summer."

"That sounds perfect, Kat."

Kat smiled her first real smile in a long time. I was desperately hoping that her old enthusiasm would return, and I caught a glimmer of it now in her eyes. I felt a great sense of relief to have a plan, any plan, to dull this constant grief inside. When the taxi arrived, we directed him to pick up Katie. She had been so confident that I would like the plan that she came out waving three bus tickets in her hand. We all hugged and danced as we loaded her things into the taxi. We had a short wait at the bus station. When the big silver bus pulled in, we boarded it, wide-eyed and excited. We were on our way to Roanoke, Virginia.

Chapter Nineteen

Mrs. Crank was determined to have a successful party. Planning it seemed to invigorate, rather than weary, her. She lined up a band, spotlighted in the Sunday paper. The band, Blues Down Under, sang a wide selection of blues and jazz. The band consisted of one female vocalist and two men. Mrs. Crank mentioned that in her youth she had sung the blues often. With her, I never knew if the remark was to be taken at face value. She was pleased that Alba had agreed to come. She kept giving me lists of things to order. Her excitement was contagious and the other residents volunteered to assist, if needed. Mrs. Crank was still working on her guest list. She had an odd assortment of friends from all walks of life. The party would be held the following Saturday, so I took the lists home to start work on immediately. Kat and Katie dropped by and offered to help. Katie was depressed. Her visit with her mother had not gone well. The trip down with Mandy was one disaster after the next. Mandy had refused to help pay expenses. She said she needed her money to live on in Florida. Her personalities had reigned, providing chaos and tricks throughout the trip. By the time they arrived at the Mama's house, Katie was a nervous wreck. They unloaded Mandy's things. When Katie started into the house with her bag, Mama had pointedly blocked her way. She told her she could not come in until she knew how to behave like a decent human being.

"Mama, please!" Katie pleaded. "I am exhausted and broke."

"Those are tribulations that you bring upon yourself," Mama said. Then she slammed the door and locked it.

Katie screamed and pounded on the door, but Mama refused to acknowledge her. Finally she gave up and started home. She ran out of gas in Knoxville, Tennessee. Katie pawned her rings, but still barely had enough to coast home. Kat was upset at the cruelty of it all, but Katie was tentatively trying to make excuses for Mama's behavior. It doesn't matter how bad a parent gets, sometimes a child just cannot accept the reality of rejection. Katie wanted to please her mother but the bars were set too high. She never made it through the hoops. As much abuse as Katie had experienced, she still longed for her mother's love. With no idea left of how to comfort Katie, I directed her toward the Internet to help with ordering the party supplies. Kat pulled a chair up beside the desk to help out. Katie was not ready to be distracted.

"Why can't Mama love me," she asked. "She loves the others. She even loves Mandy, and Mandy has all those personalities. Your mama can't love you two because she's dead, but mine is alive."

"She can't love anyone," Kat said. "She is totally involved in herself and her ego. She's a control freak. Some people aren't cut out to be parents, but they get to be anyway. They resent it, but they're also too worried about what the world will say to give the kid away. So they keep the kid, and it pays the price for interfering with their interest in themselves."

"If I had the Alabama Crystal, if I had been born with it in the family, I would have been happier and able to change things."

"The crystal is lost," Kat said. "Forget about it."

"I wish I had something magical to change things in my life."

"You do," Kat said. "it's called initiative, ambition, and hard work. That's the real magic. Believing in yourself. Trying things, and if you mess up, trying them again and again."

"She loves the others," Katie said in a small voice, everything she was hearing skipping over her head.

"She does not love the others. They're no more lovable than you are," Kat said. "She simply loves that they are under her complete control. "

"Mandy's not under anyone's control," Katie said.

"Mandy is a broken doll your mama wants to keep hidden at home. She was a beautiful gift that your mama broke and tries to hide."

"We love you, Katie," I said.

"I love you guys, too," she said in a very tired voice.

They left shortly afterwards and I sat thinking of the crystal. I knew that Kat should be told about the Alabama Crystal. When it had disappeared so long ago, we had resigned ourselves to its loss with a great deal of guilt over our failure to find it. Over the years, we talked about it a great deal, but never arrived at any explanation of its disappearance. Now it was in my possession. I had used the crystal after the fire and intended to give it to Kat. I pulled it from its hiding place. It was really very plain without sunlight. Perhaps the beauty could only shine through when the crystal was used. When Kat called to talk, I asked to come over. I told her I had something important to tell her.

"You aren't sick, are you?" she asked instantly. I told her that I had something to show her and that she would be surprised. She said she'd be by as soon as she dropped off some pastries at the community center. I stood looking out my back window at the mountains in the distance. I could not understand how the crystal made its way back after so many years. It was hard to imagine what hands it had traveled through.

Kat arrived looking small and tired. She was still concerned about Katie and the way Katie's mother had treated her when she had tried to visit. The mother controlled Mandy to a significant degree. She even encouraged and attempted to control the personalities. I knew the entire situation made Kat feel helpless.

"What do you have to show me," Kat asked.

I held the crystal out in the palm of my hand. Katie stared at it for a moment, then looked at me in confusion.

"Where did you find the Alabama Crystal?"

"I didn't find it, it found me," I said, and told her about the envelope. We both knew that the crystal was supposed to be hers on her wedding day, but there were things that Aunt El could not foresee. It belonged with Kat.

"But it has Aunt El's name on it. Why? How can it be? Are you sure it is the real crystal?"

"Yes," I said, "very sure." It lay dully in my hand. I held it to the light and it sparkled in a warm glow.

"The crystal belongs to you now. I really don't know how it found us, but I do know that it is yours. You can do whatever you wish with it."

"I don't know what to do with it," she said. "I can't understand who sent it and why they used Aunt El's name."

"I know," I said. "And it's also her handwriting. I know she didn't send it, but I also know that the handwriting is uniquely hers."

I handed Kat the small teakwood box. I felt the sadness of loss. I loved the feeling that the crystal had given me—the connection to Aunt El and the hope that it seemed to inspire. Whatever happened to the crystal now, whatever Kat decided to use it for, would be her decision alone. She stood staring at it a long time.

Chapter Twenty

We were fortunate to arrive in Roanoke in the spring. The trip up was an adventure in itself. Watching the tall, fat-topped trees across the flat expanse of sandy soil that turned into clay marshes and then to foothills was like walking through a painting that continued to change canvases. The small hills of North Carolina grew larger. Finally the mountains stood purple in the distance. Up close, soft fern, Indian paints, and tiny violets dotted the hills that rolled upwards from the highway as we sped along. I felt the odd sensation of living inside of a watercolor. Everything stood still in a soft gray fuzz as we sped past. In the higher passages of road, we could look down and see the fog, floating in cotton waves across the treetops. We were impressed with the cool breezes and lack of humidity. The mountains rolled as we climbed to higher altitudes, from deep greens into blues, and purples in the distance. It was an alien world. Seemingly endless hills on each side of us. I felt that we were rising above our past. We were being propelled upwards and away from all that was familiar, but it was exciting and invigorating. We yearned to experience new things.

As the bus entered Roanoke, we were awed by the huge buildings and the large number of colorful restaurants. It was the biggest city we had ever traveled to. So many people and all of them moving so fast, as though they had vital destinations that must be reached quickly. I'm sure we looked like the country girls we were, pointing and exclaiming over signs and shops. The bus stopped with a scream of brakes and the door seemed to heave open with exhaustion into noise, greetings, and huge numbers waiting to board the bus or to greet those descending from it.

Katie's friend, Lacy, met us at the bus station. Katie met her on her travels in her teen years and they kept in touch through letters. Lacy was an exotic creature to Kat and I. We had never crossed the Georgia line. The school we attended had a strict dress code. We wore matching skirts and sweater sets, our hair curled under, and our faces free of make up. I tried once to wear a pair of slacks to school, but was promptly sent home to change. Lacy was beautiful. She wore jeans and a long, golden glitter shirt with a matching headband across her forehead. Her eyes were large and dark, in excellent contrast to her long, golden hair. She wore brown sandals that revealed her toes, each painted a different color. She and Katie squealed and hugged. She turned and included Kat and myself in the hug.

"You will love it here," she said. "School doesn't start back until fall, so I have lots of time to show you around. I work the night shift at Pizza Place, and sleep late, but after that I am all yours."

The town looked huge to me as we hurried by large old buildings with balconies, and a couple of sleek, newer ones. Finally we arrived at Maple Street, tree lined, with small white houses. They all appeared very similar.

Buttercups, irises, and golden rods bloomed in the front yards. When we reached Lacy's house, I was happy to see beautiful peach, red, and yellow tulips already announcing the season. Aunt El loved flowers, and the tulips held a hint of her presence. Inside the house was a kitchen, den, and two bedrooms. Boxes and a variety of items were pushed against the wall in one. I could see that Lacy had tried to make room for us. Both bedrooms had mattresses on the floor and pink sheets at the windows. The windows were raised and air lifted the curtains with magical fingers. I felt happy and free. If we were to make a fresh future, this was both a peaceful and exciting place to start. Still, it felt strange to be on my own, and I was sure Kat felt the same way. Katie and Lacy planned to share one room, and Kat and I the other. I was pleased to have my sister in the same room. There had been so many changes already. Lacy ordered a large pizza for dinner, and prepared an excellent salad to accompany it. She said we could take turns cooking. Kat was happy with that. She loved to create dishes, mostly so she could name them. We had seldom eaten pizza and I relished each bite. Kat studied the pizza carefully. I could tell that she was storing its construction in her mind. It was an exotic wheel of delight.

Kat and Katie cleared the salad bowls as Lacy and I tried to find places for the extra luggage. Later the three of us fell asleep as soon as Lacy left for her job. The low hum of the fan lulled us all to our dreams. The next morning we woke up anxious to explore. Our first stop was the bank, where I deposited the inheritance. We still had the majority of the thousand in cash left. Since it was the beginning of the month, we paid Lacy a hundred and fifty dollars for rent. The house rented for two hundred, which was due in a few days. We offered money on the utilities, but Lacy said to wait until the following month. She was thrilled to have someone share the expenses. She said she seldom had anything left over from her paycheck. She wanted to show us the university where she attended school. It was a huge campus. At one spot in the road, you could look down and see the entire layout. The old brick buildings were surrounded by greenery. The mountains enclosed everything protectively. She also took us shopping. I asked her to suggest stores, and she was happy to do so. Kat, Katie, and I purchased hip huggers, white belts, smock tops, and sandals. I found a purple bubble shirt, Kat insisted on the American flag pullovers, and Katie grabbed a mini skirt. We had our ears pierced at a little shop that offered it free with the purchase of earrings. We stopped at a coffee shop for a Coke and to meet a friend of Lacy's who worked there. His name was Dylan McKeen.

"Black Irish," he said, grinning, as we were introduced. His hair and eyes were dark, his face friendly and masculine. As we were leaving, he followed us to the door. He told Lacy he was planning to drop by later.

"I see you're anxious to know my new roommates," she laughed.

"I am," he said, with a slow smile, "if that's cool with you."

"Come on, Romeo," someone shouted from the back. We laughed and headed home. I could feel Dylan's eyes on us as we walked away. When I turned to look, he was staring at Katie, her head flung back in laughter, her hands moving in a lively description of something she had noticed. Katie had another admirer to add to her list.

Chapter Twenty-One

Once the Alabama Crystal had been delivered to Kat, I felt a sense of completion and relief. I also felt a strong urge to see Doc. Not only had my panic attacks become more frequent, but a sense of grief long since buried put in an appearance. The crystal brought back so many memories of Aunt El. Her selfless dedication to those she loved, taking responsibility, not only for her sister, but also for her two orphaned nieces. My mind drifted back to the fire. The look on her face when she said that the crystal held no magic. She seemed possessed with a desperate emphasis, a great passion that we understand something. Perhaps she was trying to say that we make our own luck, that the crystal was really the parts of us that continued to strive against great odds.

It was growing dark outside. Katie called and asked me to join them at the local Italian restaurant. They were having a karaoke contest. I didn't want to be alone, so I drove on over. The girls waved from a side booth, and I excused myself through the crowd and joined them. Katie had a huge book of songs that she was scanning carefully. There's a sort of code to karaoke. You must be careful not to pick a song that you know from experience is the solid property of someone else. In other words, the one they're known by. Kat was leaning over her shoulder.

"How about this one?" she said.

"Nope," Katie replied, "Jeannie is singing that one."

"Oh, yeah, I forgot," Kat said.

"When do we go up?"

"I am not sure," Katie said. "I think after this next guy."

A group of girls were giggling their way through *Just A Swinging'* Everyone gave them a hand and the DJ called up the next voice. A young guy stepped up and crooned through a popular love song.

"Man, he was good," Katie said. "I hate to follow him."

"We don't have to," Kat said, pointing to a tall, thin woman making her way to the mic. The woman began rendering her version of *Build Me Up Buttercup*. I thought it was an odd choice. It is also a song of nuances and varying keys, a fact that the woman failed to acknowledge. She sang straight through, line by line, in monotone. If she possessed any degree of enthusiasm, it had long since crept up to the bar for a drink. When she finished singing, everyone applauded vigorously. It was a polite group.

"Good," Katie said. "Following her will make us sound that much better."

Kat and Katie belted out their song, *Bobby McGee*. Kat had the uncanny ability to mimic Joplin's high growl. Katie came off sultry and sweet. It was right on key. For that fact alone, the group was wild with enthusiasm. They sat back down, satisfied. Katie went straight back to the book. I was looking around to find the waitress. She appeared in a few minutes.

"Here," she said, thrusting a drink in my hand and taking the money I extended. She seemed irritated that we had expectations of her. She stalked off in a sullen pout.

"That's her boyfriend over there," Katie whispered. "He's hitting on that blonde woman. She needs to pretend it doesn't bother her!"

"She needs to contact lost and found and see if anyone turned in a personality," Kat said. I stayed a couple of hours and told them I had to leave. I rode home through the quiet streets. The loud echoes from the restaurant seemed to ring in my ears, like stepping off a school bus and the sound still holds sway for a few minutes. At home I watched a movie. It was difficult to sleep. I changed the channel to the preaching network. It made me feel safe and usually lulled me into sleep. I also turned on the fan. The white noise had a soothing effect. It seemed to block out the sound of anything bad and finally let me relax.

Chapter Twenty-Two

We stayed with Lacy for a month, but things just weren't working out. Lacy, herself, was wonderful. Another friend, having difficulties with her parents, had called to ask if she could crash for a while. The house was small, and not likely to grow any larger, so we decided to find a place of our own. It was fun to look around. We discovered various spots that we planned to return to. We looked for several days. One day we stopped to look at an empty house on a lovely street. The house had sliding doors and a patio. Through the windows, we could see a fireplace and wood floors.

We called the number from the sign on the lawn. The house was not for rent, but the owner was offering it for sale. We were young and the thought of buying seemed daunting. We had not considered buying a house. Suddenly it seemed like a good idea. The real estate agent took care of everything.

In less than five days, we were in the house. It was in both of our names. Now, if we had nothing else, we had a house completely paid for. It made both of us feel secure. We loved the area. Most of all, we loved knowing that, no matter where we roamed, we had a home to return to. The house consisted of three bedrooms, one huge bathroom, dining room, living room, and the basement, which was only partly finished. The walls were cement and the ceiling corkboard. We kept it locked off because, so far, we had nothing to store. The house cost $30,000. A refrigerator and stove came with it, but that was the extent of our furnishings. Lacy suggested we try the Goodwill store. Often when the students returned home, emptying their dorm rooms, they left behind or donated pieces of furniture no longer wanted or needed. Kat and I didn't mind if the items were used. With Katie by our side we searched the Goodwill Store. Kat picked out a small daybed and two twin beds. They weren't a set, but we didn't care about that, either. I chose an overstuffed dark green chair with, for once, a matching loveseat, and a small dining table with four wooden chairs. Lacy had one of her friends bring a truck over and haul our purchases back to the house for us. We also bought two beanbag chairs, an antique clock, and drapes. We stopped by the store for bed linens. The patio out back had lovely small violets and daffodils around it. The previous owners had left behind the outdoor lounge set, black wrought iron, with firm cushions. We were so focused on furnishings that we had forgotten food, but Lacy and Katie went back out while Kat and I put together and made beds, returning with four large bags of groceries and a bottle of red wine to celebrate. Kat and I were long to fall asleep. It was our first night in our new home, and we were excited. Most of all, we felt secure once again.

Chapter Twenty-Three

Alba overcame her irritation over the failed séance by having another one. This time it was to be at my house, and her brightest hope was that a ghost would materialize. She was still convinced that her peace of mind was sacrificed to odd odors. This time she was wary of the smell of flowers. That she owned a room full of them did nothing to calm her fears, because it was a certain kind of flower that she smelled. One she did not own, but which was somehow "vaguely" familiar.

She dumped the checked tablecloth for a black, lacy version with a more authentic gravity to it because, she said, "Everyone knows death likes black."

She also strung up a huge dream catcher directly over the center of the table to trap bad spirits. She only wanted nice ghosts, and assumed that if they smelled like flowers, they would be. Once more I rang up my faithful sister and friends.

"Oh, brother," Kat said, "why do you indulge her?"

"She seems sincerely convinced. There are lots of unanswered questions in the world. I've never seen a ghost, but who knows? And it will ease her mind."

"What mind?" Kat said, but she promised to be there.

Alba was arranging candles, and graciously explaining damnation and being held to earth for a purpose. She had such a zeal for her plan that I found myself actually hoping a ghost might materialize, if only for her satisfaction.

"The girls will be over in about an hour," I said.

"Good," Alba nodded, "With our energies combined, we should alert the spirit world. I know that someone up there is trying to tell me something."

"Okay," I said. "Anyway, I need to take a shower. Just let yourself out or stay here. I won't be but a minute."

I came out in ten minutes, but Alba was gone. I ground some African coffee beans, and sat down to wait. Kat and Katie arrived early, but Darrie had to work late.

"I see we're going all out this time," Kat said, rolling her eyes at the black tablecloth and candles. She hit the dream catcher lightly and it swung.

"Beware of touching that!" Alba said loudly from the doorway.

"Damn!" Kat said. "What is your problem? I barely touched it."

"The concern is for you," Alba said anxiously, "Bad spirits are trapped inside of that thing! I don't want them to enter your flesh."

"Thank you for the concern," Kat said politely.

"I wouldn't touch it," Katie said. "I've witnessed bad spirits in my own house!" She loved to throw herself into anything with enthusiasm.

"That was your ex," Kat said dryly.

"Okay" I said brightly, "let's get this show on the road."

"This is not a show, Sylvie," Alba said in a steady voice. "What you all witness here tonight must never leave this room."

"Trust me, I won't tell a soul," Kat said.

"Me, either," Katie interjected, "because they'd think we're a bunch of idiots." She was a little too direct, causing the eye of Alba to turn balefully toward her.

"Well," I said, "let's take a seat and try to help Alba. Everyone listen to everything she tells you to do."

Alba was appeased. Being in charge was her favorite position, so she took a seat and we all followed nicely.

First she lit the candles, while humming softly under her breath what sort of kind of sounded like an Indian chant. I could only make out aw wa wa chou, or something along those lines. Everything was flickering in the candlelight and from the nearby street light. Eerie shadows played at the window when the wind brushed the trees outside.

Finally, Alba stopped humming and got down to business.

"Oh, ancestors," she suddenly bellowed, "Oh, virtuous men and women of gentle compliance and goodwill, give heed to our cry and distinguish proof of the flowered ghost that rises up to give warning! Come forward, oh, ancestors and help us pursue the cause and reason of this affliction that calls out through a flower for justice!"

Wow, I thought, she must have been practicing!

"It's a Lilac," she said loudly, in case the ancestors were deaf, I suppose. "It's a purple lilac of sweet bloom that imparts a prayer to be heard. What does the spirit want, oh, Ancestor?"

We all sat quietly a good five minutes. Obviously, her ancestors were a little slow. Then suddenly the table started to shake, rattle, and roll. Okay, not roll, but you get the picture. Something was happening. I could see the amazement on Katie and Kat's face. Kat looked under the table in case Alba had planted some kind of device.

"Thank you, Ancestor," Alba said a bit smugly.

Then a soft voice drifted through Alba's mouth. "It is there with you," said the ancestor,

"The reason lies there with you in the gold of evidence." Then everything stopped abruptly. Alba was sweating. She waited, but nothing else seemed to be forthcoming from the spirit world. Katie jumped up and turned on the lights.

"Whoa, what was that with the table?" she said.

"I don't know," Alba said. "Can any of you decipher the message we received?" No one could think of anything to say.

"'The reason is here in the gold of evidence'. What does it mean? Why are we being haunted? That is still unanswered."

"Excuse me," said Kat, "but you're the one being haunted. I can walk around all day and never smell the flowers."

"Undoubtedly true," said Alba. Sometimes she reminded me of Kat.

"I want to go home," Katie said. "This is spooky and weird. Who lifted the table?"

It was a good question. A good one to end the séance on, too. The girls left, but Alba lingered.

"Do you know what they could have meant? The spirit sounded sad," Alba said.

"I have no idea," I said honestly.

"Sylvia, there is something here that has aroused the other world. Do you know what it could be?"

"No," I said. "Maybe it was a scent that drifted in off the streets. You do keep your windows open."

"After what went on here tonight, you still doubt me?" Alba was offended.

"I don't know what to think. I believe something happened, but it has to do with you, Alba. We're just here for moral support."

"No," she said firmly, "it reacted here differently than it did in my basement. I know now that it involves all of us."

With continual bouts of panic attacks looming more and more often, the last thing I needed was involvement with the spirit world. I could barely stay normal in this one.

"Let's just call it a night, Alba. I'll think about it and we will talk later."

"All right," she said, gathering all her séance fixings and walking stiffly out the door.

"Goodnight."

Chapter Twenty-Four

Finally it was my day with Doc. I needed to see him. I also needed a Bloody Mary, but it was too early in the day. I wore a long sleeved shirt and long skirt to therapy. Sometimes I had this thing about revealing too much of myself. Nothing like a big coverall of clothing to help conceal things.

"Dressed a little warmly today, aren't you?" he said knowingly.

"I guess so," I said. "I catch cold easily."

"Hmm," he said.

I could see by the furrow of his brow and sad eyes that his son was home from college. It was his first year away at school. It was also his first year with divorced parents. Doc's ex loved to call the boy at school and tell him that his father was in the counting house counting all his gold, while she suffered. Though never in silence. The boy, already upset by the divorce, plus being a money-loving teen with a surly personality, resented his dad immensely. I picked most of this information up waiting for a card for my next appointment. Secretaries often believe they are dealing with the deaf and dumb. Anyway, that was the secret of the furrowed brow.

"You left pretty quickly last week," Doc said.

"Yes, I was having a panic attack."

"It was nice of you not to worry me with it," he said. He could be a bit sarcastic, but I like sarcastic men.

"I'm sorry. It is just that I have to move very quickly when I panic."

"What do you think caused it," he asked.

That is when I told him about the Alabama Crystal. The entire history as I knew it. When I finished, he looked thoughtful for a minute or two.

"I believe your panic has to do with the crystal," he said. "Perhaps it involves a fear you have for Kat. After all, Aunt El did behave oddly, furiously, you said, in condemning the crystal. Why do you think that was?"

"I have no idea. Well, actually I have an idea, but I'm not sure. I think she turned against the crystal because of Lily's death," I said.

"That could be," he said thoughtfully, "but what about the baby? She asked for a safe delivery, but wasn't it a huge cruelty that the crystal gave her what she asked for, and then took her only child? To her, the crystal may have appeared to be a huge jokester." I could see the sense in what he was saying. I had never considered how severe the blow must have been to her. Fortunately, she had Lily, and then Kat and I to fill the void. But could your own child ever be replaced?

"You haven't had a panic attack for some time. The crystal shows up and you have one," he said calmly, as though urging a reluctant child to good reasoning. We talked for a long while, and then I told Doc that I needed to think.

"Are you sure you don't need to talk more?"

"Thank you, Doc, but, no, I need to go, I only have ten minutes left anyway, No need to get into anything else." I smiled to show him I was fine. He raised his brows, but smiled back. I was troubled by his interpretation of the crystal and the fact it might have represented pain to Aunt El. He was right about my panic also. It had been a while since my last attack, but with the crystal there, things seem to speed toward crisis in my mind. My faith in the crystal had soared when the healing that I requested for the three of us had occurred so quickly. It was all troubling to me. I arrived home, emotional exhaustion heavy in my body and thoughts.

Alba was at the door almost as soon as I pulled it shut behind me.

"I don't want to barge in," she said, "but I've been smelling the flowers this morning and they lead straight to this door. It is as though the spirits need me to speak to you." I was too tired to talk with Alba, and definitely too tired to speak to spirits.

"There is something about lilacs; that is the scent that leads me here. Yes, yes, the smell is strongest here," she continued. "Do you know anyone who could be trying to contact any of us with lilacs?" I shifted uneasily.

"Think," she commanded.

"Aunt El loved lilacs beyond any bloom," I said, "but she isn't the type to haunt my neighbors. I'm sure she would come directly to me. Listen, Alba, I'm not sure what is going on with you, but we have been friends a long time. Maybe you need some medication for your nerves."

"Look," she said urgently, "I should have told you this a long time ago. There is a thin line between the other side and this one. I have the ability to see the future. I haven't mentioned it simply because I was afraid you'd react this way. If you'd condescend to listen, I could tell you many things."

I felt my head start to ache in a slow throbbing heartbeat. I could see red lights behind my eyes. I longed to find a darkened room and collapse away from the sharp points of light that seemed to surround me.

"Sylvia," she said, "there are so many things I could teach you."

"Okay, I appreciate it, Alba, but I'm going to lie down now."

"It's because your head is aching and you are emotionally drained," she said wisely.

I couldn't see that it took much psychic ability to come to that conclusion. I could feel my eyes squinting now. The light was like an atomic glare. I could barely stand to keep my eyes open another moment. Alba finally realized that it would be best to leave.

"We will talk later," she said with disappointment. I dropped onto the couch.

"Okay," I said. "Okay." Then I fell asleep, unaware of when she left. I drifted into a dream. It was a dream that I'd experienced often. I did not want to see the symbolism or intent of it. I only wanted it to go away. In the dream I sat in a circle of women. They were passing a bundled baby around the circle. Each woman spent a moment admiring the baby. Each one cooed playfully into the blanket. I could see dark hair. Finally the baby reached my arms. I stared down smiling and then began to scream. The baby had no face. There was only smooth skin where the face should be.

I woke up crying. The dream troubled me. I did not want to know what it meant. I did not want dreams. I sat outside on the patio. The sun appeared to be rising slowly and shyly in a coral reach of light. I watched it for a long time. The fingers of the sun seemed to strike through the dark trees like the light of insight into a clouded mind. I went inside and dressed for the day.

Chapter Twenty-Five

Katie fell for Dylan McKeen the first moment she met him. Of course, she didn't tell us until later. Later consisted of about two months. She and Dylan went to South Carolina to be married. She wanted to travel on down to show off her new husband to, well, you guessed it, her mother. During her brief time and distance away, Mama had suddenly morphed into a pleasant memory. Who knows how, but that's love, and need, and family, and how it works out pretty often. We gave her money for a bus ticket, should things go wrong with Dylan. She was offended, but not stupid, so she took it. She said if things went well for a week, she'd cash it in. We all liked Dylan; he was fun to talk to, and very handsome. But he was player, and one of the things he liked to play with, besides women, happened to be cocaine. Katie was quick to his defense.

"He only uses it because it helps with the pain when his football knee acts up," she explained. "Anyway, we'll be back here in a month. We both have some money saved from work."

She had started working with Dylan a couple of weeks after we arrived. We did the only thing we could do, which was wish her well and congratulate them both. With Katie gone, Kat decided to go to school with Lacy. I'd been suggesting it for weeks. The university was expensive, so only one of us could attend. I wanted it for Kat very badly. She had a genius mind. Lacy helped her with all the forms and even applied for the two of them to work part-time at the cafeteria.

"Are you unselfishly giving up school for me," Kat asked suspiciously.

"No," I said, honestly, "I don't want to go. I have a high school diploma and I've applied for a job with a community action agency."

The agency worked with the children in low-income families. They had already confided that I would definitely be hired, but it would be a week before they opened the daycare. My job would be to teach the four-year-olds. I was very anxious to start. A week later I was called in to work.

September in the mountains was beautiful. The leaves, with their various sizes and shapes, created a spectacular panorama that rolled in orange, red, burgundy, and yellow across the ridges. The air would begin to cool, and the smell of wood smoke from the stoves common in most homes where we lived, rose to blend with the breezes.

Even the animals, growing their thick winter coats, seemed to gleam as they graze. I knew that many people felt too closed in to live in the mountains, but I thought that the hills offered a sense of security. To me, it was more that things were locked out, not that I was locked in. I loved traveling just outside of the city limits to the small school in the valley. The children were loud, full of life, and glad to have playmates. I had never been around many children and found that I had a natural affinity with them. I loved their fresh, un-jaded view of the world. They loved the clay, the huge crayons, the slides, and the merry go round. Even the shyest of them, the ones who cried at first for their mothers, seem to grow quiet as I spoke soothingly, whispering of magic games that we might play.

With Katie still away, Kat and Lacy were together constantly. Kat loved her job at the cafeteria, and grew very popular on campus for her quick wit and humor. She was taking a heavy load of classes and appeared to be filling out forms or schedules endlessly the first two weeks of the first semester. September and October flew by in a brilliant array of autumn leaves. I was contented with the children, making handprints and pasting leaves. Katie returned from her extended honeymoon. She and Dylan asked to stay with us until they could find jobs, since their prolonged absence, apparently without permission from their employer, had left them without work. They piled their things in the guest room. The visit with her mother had been anything but a success, and Katie was sad and still disowned by her family.

Kat stayed over with Lacy often. She said it was easier access to school and the various friends they had on campus. She seemed busy and happy.

In November, Lacy announced that she was quitting school. She left with one of her girlfriends for Colorado. Lacy said they had a job there waiting for them. They planned to work on a ranch that provided free lodging and a weekly paycheck for labor. It was difficult to picture Lacy as a ranch hand. She laughed and explained that her friend would be working around the ranch and that she would be a maid and cook. It seemed a great distance from the life she had now, but she was restless.

They also planned to stop at a commune out west. Lacy's leaving devastated Kat. She grew more and more despondent and began cutting classes. Finally, she locked herself in her room for hours at a time. She had many friends at the university and I was constantly urging her to spend more time with them, but to no avail.

A great deal of my time, outside of work, was spent with one of the teachers at the daycare. He was a single, older man in his thirties, and was teaching me some new methods of study that he practiced with the children. His name was Bradley Hilton, but he asked me to call him Buck. He was tall, with broad shoulders, and a slim waist. His hair was curly and he tried to control it by brushing it straight back. His eyes were dark blue. He was well known for his gentle nurturing ways with the children. We spent more and more time together. I suppose it was inevitable that we fell in love. It was my first romance and I was lost in daydreams of Buck. I fell asleep at night thinking of him. He assured me that it was the same with him, and that my face was always the last thing he remembered when he went to bed. He asked me to spend the weekend with him. He owned a beautiful cabin in the valley. We made love for the first time as the water rushed by outside the window. I loved to lay and look at him and trace his face and brow line with my fingers.

I spent the weekend laughing and holding on to Buck at every possible moment. I returned home on Sunday to find Kat more depressed than ever. She had not realized I had been away. She had lost weight and her eyes were dark circled and tired. Katie and Dylan tried to cheer her up with invitations to join them in town. She never wanted to leave the house.

I wanted to introduce Buck to Kat and Katie, but he insisted that we keep our love a secret for the time being. He said it was frowned upon for teachers to develop a relationship. After the first time, we made love as often as possible. Often Buck would have drinks waiting when I arrived at his cabin. I had difficulty staying alert. I discovered that I had a low tolerance for alcohol. Buck drank a great deal. When he drank, he laughed a great deal and told wonderful stories of adventures he had experienced in the past. Buck had seminars out of town once a week. He always returned whistling, lifting me off my feet, and onto the bed. I always called ahead when I visited him. He insisted on it, so that he could prepare one of his gourmet meals.

One day I could not call because the phone lines were being repaired. I stopped at the restaurant in town for food to take to the cabin. I wanted to surprise him with a prepared lunch. I was the one destined to be surprised. I pulled into the drive and saw Buck chopping wood. When he saw me, he hurried over. I jumped out and flung my arms around him. He stiffened and pulled away. Two young children came dashing out from behind the cabin. A pretty woman in a parka followed behind them. He approached them quickly and put his arms around the woman.

"This is my wife, Lynn, and these are my two children." He gave me a pleading look. "This is the teacher I told you about," he said to his wife. "She is learning some of the new methods for the classroom."

His wife smiled and asked if I would like to stay for lunch. I couldn't think of anything to say. I told her I was looking for ginseng and had to hurry on, which I immediately did. I glanced in my rearview mirror. They stood waving, a small family waving at a stranger. An unreal horror and grief consumed me.

When I arrived home sobbing, Kat blinked, as though awakening from a trance. She put her arms around me and I told her the entire story. She looked sick with sadness for me. I fell asleep that night in Kat's bed. Love has the ability to clear fields with a wide blade; sometimes they lie as a gleaming clean harvest, and sometimes as sharp, pointed stubble. In our house, the failures in love fell like a disease, and the contagion touched everyone.

While Kat and I huddled in devastation, Katie and Dylan were stumbling the uneasy path of passion and hasty marriage. In their case, a marriage of opposites might have proven more beneficial. Their downfall lay in their compatibility, for neither of them really wished to be responsible for anyone but themselves. They each enjoyed outgoing, laid back personalities. They were both hoping that the other would provide stability and balance. They were also both hoping that the other would work. Without jobs, they became restless and angry. They were unable to afford even the smallest necessities. When they spoke of pictured happiness, their words were always evocative of earlier times, before they met and married. Eventually, both of them began seeking fulfillment elsewhere, and the short marriage stumbled and fell. Dylan disappeared easily into his former life, but Katie's head still rang with her mother's predictions of failure. Kat revealed that she was in love with Lacy, and could not tolerate seeing the places that they had enjoyed together. Katie and I were astonished at the announcement.

"That's why you've been so depressed?" Katie asked.

"Yes," Kat said. "I was afraid to tell either one of you. I couldn't believe it myself until I saw Lacy kiss a girl at school."

"Lacy is a lesbian," Katie said. "How could we have missed that?"

"It is not something that she advertises," Kat said. "It's not the easiest thing to be. Her parents have no idea, either, just as you two didn't know about me. We were so happy together until that girl came back to school. Now I'll never see her again. Every place I go here makes me remember her."

"I still can't believe you're a lesbian," Katie said.

"Well, I can't believe that you sleep with every man you meet, but I don't go on and on about it, do I?" Katie looked hurt.

"I'm sorry, Katie," Kat said, "but sometimes you can be so irritating."

"I just want to be loved," Katie said.

"I know," Kat replied, "but you never give anyone a chance to love you. They don't know you want love because you come at them with so much sex." Now Katie fell into the slump with the two of us.

A house of depressed, lovesick women is an unpleasant place to be. It is also a hard place to survive. The world does not pause for passion or grief. The bills continue to come along, and morning breaks regardless of the circumstances or desires of an individual. With everyone in a state of pain and apathy, the house was an unkempt castle. The cold breezes of life pressed in on every side and we gave way to the frigid numbing. No one wanted to leave the house, no matter how cold, because it was the only security we had. Still, in the spring, Kat and I put the house up for sale. The times, outside of our own, were good, and we actually made a profit on the sale.

The one thing that we agreed on was that we loved the mountains. We searched the newspapers and ads until we found a house for sale in Ashford, a hundred miles away, but still in Virginia. Kat and I went there and secured the sale. Ashford was a historical, artistic town filled with monuments to fallen heroes, and trails dating back to the Trail of Tears.

The house we found was situated well inside the city limits. It was a two story, split foyer, in a circle of the same. The yard was filled with shrubbery and flowers. Pines drooped on one side and pink dogwoods on the other. Of course, Katie moved with us.

When we moved in, the house next door still proclaimed the realtor's sign. Then suddenly it was gone, and a week later, I noticed signs of activity. I didn't have time to wonder about it, as the new owner made a sudden appearance, introducing herself as Alba Smith. She was a retired administrator from a food supply company. Like us, she was enamoured of the mountains, and loved all the seasons. She was older, with an upswept hair, and a conservative style. She was also a fantastic cook, a fact well proven by the casserole and pie she carried over to meet us.

Usually it was the other way around, and we should have welcomed her first, but we were still the recovering addicts of love, although youth was quickly taking care of much of the residue. I swiftly put Kat on the job of a return gesture of goodwill. She whipped up a special Coconut Surprise cake that would've impressed Betty Crocker. It was Aunt El's recipe.

Alba proved to be very helpful. Together, we scouted the city and introduced ourselves to a few people. Alba had a private income, so she wasn't looking for work, but I followed up on a position that Alba pointed out in the paper. It was at a retirement home. The job details called for a companion of sorts.

Kat was hired at a bakery. It was a large place and she was given a spot on the production line. Katie, in her rattled, ragged car, was busy searching for a mechanic. She found Billy Mac, and he offered her a reasonable price for repairs. She also found a job in a restaurant. More of a truck stop, really, where the food was served in iron skillets, and the customers moved in and out fast, but returned at a steady rate. I tried to tuck Buck neatly into a file in my brain. I imagine Kat and Katie were trying to do the same with their own memories.

All in all, it was a beautiful time of year, and all around us, fresh starts were raging. We raged, too. My application was accepted and I became a companion to Mrs. Briar. She had no children. She was a true extrovert, with a wonderful sense of humor. The pay was excellent and the work hardly qualified as work at all, more like visiting a favorite grandmother or aunt. The job was only on weekends, Friday through Sunday, as Mrs. Briar was very ambulatory and prone to rambling about with a male friend through the week. She said that her house was ripe with memories, and that, to make a future, she needed a new starting point. She sold her house, which was difficult to maintain, and lived in the retirement home for a flat rate. She was often visited by a friend, Mrs. Crank.

Mrs. Crank was close to Aunt El's age. She was a younger cousin of Mrs. Briar. Always seemingly busy with a whirlwind of activity, she also managed to keep a sharp eye out for her cousin's welfare. I enjoyed her visits to the home. All in all, things were improving for the three of us. We flung ourselves once more into life.

Chapter Twenty-Six

Sometimes I have headaches. It doesn't happen often, and they don't last for very long. They are too bright inside my head and they force me to close my eyes. An aura of blue lingers for a moment when I awaken so that everything seems to be in soft focus. I woke up to a soft tapping noise. It was steady but annoying. I sat up and glanced around for the source of the noise. There sat Mandy in the rocking chair. Each time she rocked backwards, the chair rocker tapped the floor.

"I wouldn't feel safe sleeping with the door unlocked," she said primly.

"Hey," I said, "I thought you were in Florida."

"I was," she replied. "I was having a wonderful time with Mama, but Little Sissy missed Katie. I tried to talk her out of it, but you see where I am now."

"Not with Katie," I said.

"I couldn't find her. She must be on a date." Mandy looked like a black cat, her long dark hair loose, one leg tucked beneath her, as the other pushed the chair back and forth.

"But Katie just took you home," I said.

"I told you that I am here because of Little Sissy," she said. "She kept breaking the rules and getting me in trouble with Mama. She went to bed at six but kept waking up and trying to slip downstairs. Mama was very upset."

"How did you get here?" .

"Little Sissy talks to strangers. She talked to the man at the truck stop and he gave us a ride. Are you mad?"

"No, it's okay," I said. "I was just surprised to see you again so soon."

"I'm hungry," she said.

"Okay. Come on, I'll cook something."

She followed me into the kitchen and I prepared some scrambled eggs, toast, and bacon. I fixed some hot coffee and we sat at the table eating. She was suddenly very dignified and chatty, a master of small talk. I just nodded a lot and smiled. There was really no way to know which personality I was eating with. Kat and I usually waited for Katie to tell us that.

"Mother has the stronghold of a wrestler and a sacred claim on the souls of her children. My immorality and unnatural desires create a distance between us, as I am unable to go to bed at six, or distract myself from sensual thoughts," she said thoughtfully.

"Well," I said, "I'm sorry things didn't work out for you there."

"I felt a vindication of spirit and the urge to express myself as a woman," she said.

"That is understandable," I said agreeably.

She stopped and looked left and right, then leaned in confidentially. "I got needs," she said in a gruff voice. "There ain't a damn thing to do in that town." She suddenly straddled the chair and began to eat rapidly. Her fork was clutched in her fist tightly. She looked tough and irritated. At that moment Katie interrupted our breakfast. Obviously, my swinging doors were still unlocked. She appeared to be exhausted. Her hair stuck out in unruly curls. She hated her curly hair and kept it straight as often as she could.

"Hey, Sylvie," she said. "Mandy, what are you doing here? Mama is so mad! I've been looking for you for hours. Mama called and said you disappeared and that you were probably coming here."

Katie did not get to say much more because Mandy flung herself into her sister's arms.

"I was scared. Why did you leave Little Sissy? I want to be with you, but you always run away, and you know I'm scared. She's a mean mama."

Katie is very affectionate and a sucker for the same. Mandy couldn't have looked more appealing and frightened. She actually looked exactly like a child, a very sad one.

"Little Sissy," Katie said, as if seeing her for the first time, "I'm sorry I left you, but you wanted to go home, and Mama wanted you home."

"I don't want to go back," said unhappy Little Sissy. "I want to stay with you. I thought Mama would be nice. She was not nice. I was hungry; I ate in the kitchen at eight o'clock."

Katie looked horrified, "You know that no one is supposed to roam the house at night!" she said.

"That's a stupid rule," Mandy said. Suddenly it was Katie that looked sad.

"Yes, it is a stupid rule. Little Sissy, you can stay with me. It'll be fun."

"Don't take me back there, okay?" Little Sissy seemed ready to cry.

Katie promised that she would not take her back again. I could see from her expression that she was determined not to fail Mandy.

"Thank you, Sylvie," Katie said, turning my way.

"No problem," I said. Katie grabbed Mandy's bag and started toward the door.

Thief!" a shrill voice shouted. "How dare you touch my things!" Katie handed the bag to Mandy and the two of them left.

I was putting the dishes in the sink when I heard Alba say, "Was that Mandy? What were those two doing here so early? I thought Mandy was in Florida."

"Good morning," I replied. "Yes, that was Mandy. She's back. Apparently things didn't go well in Florida. And why is everyone up so early this morning?"

"You really should lock your door," Alba said.

"I'm beginning to feel the same way," I said.

"Why are you up so early?"

"Lilacs," Alba replied. I wanted to kick myself for asking. I should have known not to, especially since I, personally, was still sleepy.

Alba continued in a secretive voice, "I was sleeping peacefully when a mild fragrance drifted by the bed. At first I was too sleepy to notice, but the scent grew stronger. I sat up and was engulfed in the smell. When I stood up the smell moved to the kitchen. I followed closely. Then I noticed that it was trash day and I had not set the can out. I opened the door, took the can to the curb, and when I turned around, the lilacs were like a force pulling me in this direction. They led me straight to your door."

"I don't smell anything," I said.

"I believe it was meant for me to come here this morning. Don't you think that it's an omen for the scent to lead me straight to your door?" she asked.

Actually, I was pondering which sort of lock to buy to replace this one, where everyone carried a key copy for their own convenience. I was musing between a hook lock and a dead bolt, but it would be rude to say so.

"An omen," I said blankly.

"A divine revelation!" she said excitedly. "A gregarious attempt to imply a void. By a void, I mean a vacant crossing over where a ghost is caught in a void of consciousness, stuck with a realization of something it stills needs to do."

I was beginning to feel irritated. I had been patient and a good listener. I was fine with Alba's ghosts, and their variety of odors, ranging from flowers to feces, but now she was trying to force the ghost upon me. I decided to be blunt with her.

"Alba, I was happier when you kept the ghostly things on your own property. I need you to keep the ghost home. I do not smell lilacs. All I smell is bacon, eggs, and coffee."

Alba was disappointed, which I felt badly about, but still, she used to only conjure up a ghostly smell once a year, sometimes twice. Now ghosts were arriving with alarming speed, and, for that matter, so were personalities.

"I hate it when you're in this mood," she said. "Not everything in life can be explained away with logic. I thought that our long friendship was cemented with more acceptance of our differences."

Now I felt badly for hurting her feelings.

"You're right," I said. "It's okay to bring the ghosts over. It's fine!"

"Well," she said, "I would think so. At least it's something real, not like those personalities that Mandy flings off and on like dresses. You never say anything to her."

I felt even worse. She was truly excited about the spirits and flowers. It was a big, lonely house, and I suppose, with enough time and loneliness, a person could dream up almost anything.

"I'm sorry," I said. "I woke up a little too early."

Alba was quick to forgive. I offered her some coffee and she seemed happy to join me. Then Kat showed up, looking for Katie, explaining that it wasn't like Katie to take off so early. I explained to her about Mandy and her unexpected arrival. I told her about the Little Sis episode.

"Oh, yes," she said, "I like Little Sis. She's very sweet and appealing."

"She was very sad this morning," I said.

"Yeah, she always gets to Katie," Kat said. "Katie thinks she should have taken better care of Mandy, but with a mother like that, I don't think anything would have made any difference."

Alba broke in and said, "Sometimes real monsters are born on this earth in human form. It can be hard to see them."

I knew what she meant. It was like the Mama and the Preacher. People expected them to be a certain way, and if they deviated, it was hard to notice, as long as they acted self-righteous. People assumed they were practicing what they preached. We talked for a while and Kat had coffee with us. She said she wanted to give Mandy and Katie a little time alone, and then she planned to visit. Katie was always so pleased to have Kat with her when Mandy was around. Katie claimed that she knew all the personalities and could handle them, but sometimes her eyes showed such heartbreak it was difficult to look into them. The Mama had shown both of them such abuse and coldness. I have no idea why she even had children, and am still amazed at how kind and compassionate Katie had remained throughout a childhood of constant rage. She said that her mother had been angry as far back as she could remember. The father was a wimp of a man, watching from the behind the mother's skirts as daughter after daughter was shredded. The older daughters had let time dull the past, but Katie and Mandy were younger, and the memories remained raw and painful. When Kat and Alba left, I dressed and headed for the post office. The day before, while I was out, the postman had tried to deliver a package. I could see by the pink receipt that the postman left that he was not bringing the package out again. It was something Mrs. Crank had ordered. When the worker brought it out for me at the post office, it was a long, oblong package. I could hardly wait to see what was inside. Usually I ordered everything for Mrs. Crank, but this was gift she had ordered herself. When I reached the home, she was watching *The Golden Girls*. She had a huge admiration for Dorothy, but felt that she and Blanche were really more alike. She liked Sophia's grit and Rose's innocence. She was delighted that the package had finally arrived. "You will never guess what this is!" she said.

"That's true," I said. "It's wrapped too oddly for me to guess."

She made a long, dramatic process of tearing off the wrapping. There was still a long flat box to pry open. I went to the kitchen and brought her a knife. She had a letter opener, but was afraid of breaking it. It was a sleek, thin one her husband had brought her from one of his many trips, made of fine crystal with her name engraved on the handle.

Finally the box was open. First she pulled out a bow. It was beautiful, carved in one long piece, from hickory. Then she removed a quiver of arrows. The quiver was fawn colored leather decorated with mutiple colors of beads in the center.

"This is all handmade," she said. "I carried it at all times when we summered on the ranch. It is one of a kind. I want you to have it. I have enjoyed it immensely. Now, you will only learn through practice, so practice all you can with this."

I was overwhelmed with the gift. I had spent a good part of my childhood longing for a bow and arrows. Now, I held the most beautiful, and most unique, I had ever gazed upon, even in pictures.

"It's wonderful, Mrs. Crank. It's something I've always wanted. Thank you so much," I said. She nodded and smiled.

"It pleases me to make you so happy. I know that you will treasure it as I did."

"Yes. It means everything," I said. It was difficult to express my feelings.

The gift was beyond any gift I had ever received, with the exception of the crystal; but nothing could compare with that.. I felt my eyes fill with tears.

Chapter Twenty-Seven

In late July of 1977, Elvis still had a month to live, Laverne & Shirley were laughing up the airways, and I was at the local bar trying to keep my eyes focused on the juke box as guys shouted out favorites. They shouted other things, too, all of them good natured, but suggestive. Kat had dropped me here to buy the hot tamales that Bob's Bar was famous for. She was picking up some wine and circling back for me. When the tamales were ready, I grabbed the bag and a Pepsi, and went outside to wait for her. Although I love tamales, I had an ulterior motive for being dropped here. I had noticed and spoken briefly with the owner's son, Frankie. I was sure he wouldn't remember me, but I hoped to accidently run into him. Just as I walked out, Frankie pulled in driving a shiny black Charger. I leaned against the brick wall, waiting for Kat and watching him park. When he jumped out, I could see he was wearing nothing but cutoffs and flip-flops. His hair was long, and reddish brown; his face was rugged, with a nose that had obviously been broken a few times. He had a warm, natural tan and large eyes. When he got close to me, he stopped, and I could see that his eyes were brownish green with golden eyelashes.

"Whoa!" he said. "What do we have here?" I shifted shyly and said hello.

"Hey, do you need a ride?" he asked.

I said, "No, thank you, but you look trustworthy."

He threw his head back with a deep laugh. "Honey," he said, "I've been called a lot of things, but trustworthy is not one of them."

"I've seen you around here. Everyone says you're a nice guy," I said. I was never glib or good with small talk. As far as that went, I'm not that great with large talk, either. I guess I'm the silent type.

He leaned in close to me and asked, "Do you want a black?" I said no. "You want a red? A 'lude? A joint?"

"No, thank you," I said politely. This made him laugh. He gestured at the Pepsi I was holding. "I guess you don't want a beer, either?" I said no again.

Just then, Kat pulled up, and I said, "My ride is here."

"Hold on a second. Do you want to go out with me? Tomorrow night?"

"Yes," I said, and told him my name and where I lived. He said he could find it.

"Hey, this is not my car, baby," he said. "I have an old wagon. I'll have to tie your door shut to keep you from falling out."

"Okay," I said, and jumped in the car with Kat.

"Who was that?" she asked.

I told her our conversation and that we had a date tomorrow.

"You have a date, and you don't even know his name," she asked?

"Well, I know it sounds bad, but he knows mine!"

The next night he arrived on time in a black paint primed station wagon.

He opened the door for me, and then grabbed a rope and pulled it across to hook to his door to hold my door shut.

He hopped in on his side and said, "You still want to go? This is a junker. If it rains, I have to pull these other two ropes to make the wipers work."

"It's a very nice vehicle," I said politely. He laughed and said, "Okay, honey."

This time he did not offer me pills or pot. "I guess you don't do drugs," was all he said.

We drove to the Holiday Inn for dinner and drinks. His was a screwdriver, mine a Pepsi. We slow danced. Everyone there seemed to know him and he shouted greetings and slapped hands with all of them. Women approached him with whispers and hugs. He only laughed louder. On the way home he smoked a joint. The fumes made me paranoid, which made him laugh harder. "A contact high," he said. "I think you have a buzz." He took me home and kissed me goodnight. "I'll be back."

"Okay," I said.

He laughed. "Good night, darling," he said. Kat was waiting up with Katie. They both looked worried.

"He looks rough," Kat said.

"Like a convict," Katie threw in.

"Well, don't worry," I told them earnestly, "he is very trustworthy."

"Oh," Kat said. "How do you know?"

"I don't know how I know," I told them honestly, "but I know. I've watched him for a couple of months. He's very big hearted and kind. Do you think I'd go out with a complete stranger? We had a wonderful time. Besides, he grew up here, his dad owns the bar and restaurant, and he has all kinds of friends." I headed for bed.

"Hey," Kat called after me, "what's his name?"

"Frankie," I said. "His name is Frankie."

I had felt the infatuation of first love with Buck, and learned of betrayal. He made everything I felt was beautiful seem like a lie, because everything he felt was dishonest. I had been wounded, like the touch of a brand to the unsuspecting calf. I remembered the pain and humiliation. With Frankie, it was totally different. Love swelled and burst inside of me again and again. Each time I saw him was like the first. He had many friends. They all commented what an odd couple we made. They called us the straight and the crazy. My upbringing had left me unprepared for the world in many ways, and drugs were of no interest to me. I was happy and loved to dance. Frankie and I were always laughing. Several times, girls walked up and asked for something to smoke or down. They would ask for whatever I was on.

"She's on a natural high," he would say, laughing when they turned away confused and convinced he was holding the good stuff out for his girl.

In a way, I imagine he was. He was a genius. I loved to listen to him talk. His voice was a deep drum and his laughter contagious. He had a charisma that drew others to him. He really listened when they spoke. I really listened when he spoke. I would lay and listen as he talked about his childhood. He was the baby in his family. Growing up in a restaurant, he'd become independent early, and would come home from school and prepare what he wanted on the grill. He loved to read, a fact that few of his friends realized. He loved history and traveling and dreamed of living at the beach. We went there often, and he was a part of the landscape. Any place we went he adapted into the environment like a native and made friends instantly. He had a quality that made people want to talk to him. We spent one summer slipping away to his friend's houseboat to make love and throw parties. We would lie awake at night, as the house boat drifted back and forth at will, listening to Jimmy Buffet and Bob Seger. He used to sing *Night Moves*, and *Running Against the*

Wind as we watched the stars. Four years after we met, I discovered I was pregnant. He worked construction out of town a great deal, but started looking closer to home. He was excited about the baby. I was happy. The doctor we'd chosen seemed to think everything was going along right on schedule. We were looking forward to being parents. When I was four months pregnant, we went to the convenience store for his cigarettes. He pulled over and said he'd be right back. He kissed me and jumped out of the car. Neither of us noticed the truck in the evening glare of sun. The truck that crushed him between itself and our car. I was knocked unconscious. When I woke up in the hospital, Kat's face told me everything. No Frankie, no baby. I slipped back into unconsciousness. I remember hoping that I would never wake up. I know that the human body often strides forward against great odds. The mind learns lessons and absorbs them in an archive of memory that throws in rational thought to even out the unbearable.

For a very long time, I was not rational. The unbearable was a wall that my eyes opened to each morning. I could not find the way to continue. Silence reigned inside of me. In the midst of crowds, I could hear the hollow sound of wind through the skeleton of flesh that I reluctantly inhabited. Kat and Katie were stunned also. No one really prepares for the destruction and chaos that death deals out. The emptiness in my life tried to fill itself with work and compassion for the elderly at the home. Because I was raw, I touched others tenderly. I became so enamoured of solitude at the end of the day that Kat began begging me to go out somewhere, anywhere, with her. Finally she began to cry. For the first time in a very long time, I thought of the Alabama Crystal. Why had I used it so young? Would it have made a difference if I had been able to draw upon it for a good long life with Frankie? I was tormented with the thought that I could, or should, have been able to prevent everything that had happened.

When the snowstorm hit our area, Kat was stranded overnight at the laundry. She made it home the next morning when the snowplows came through, but the heat had malfunctioned at the laundry and she had spent a cold night. She went to bed early and woke up the next morning with a high fever. By evening, she was delirious. The doctor diagnosed pneumonia and admitted her to the hospital. Her system was having difficulty recovering and the doctor said she had an acute case. I sat by her bed watching her flushed face. Suddenly I realized that death could make his way into my life once more. Without Kat, I would be alone. By the time she recovered from pneumonia, I had restored my will to go on. I tucked Frankie and the baby into the softest corner of my mind, and knew I would return to them often. I also knew my life would continue. I would not be the same person. No one ever really recovers, but they grasp, and adjust, and fit their life shirts on for the others that they love and the ones that love them back. I moved forward with Kat and Katie into the promise of life once again. For everything taken, something is given back. I felt that Kat's life was spared and her illness used as a reminder to still appreciate what I had with me. There would always be moments, sudden flashes of memory, when I would feel the first kick of my baby, or remember gold lashes over laughing eyes.

When Kat was well enough, we went to the beach at Boca Raton, and rented a house on stilts. The windows opened out over the endless horizon. At morning the sun rose faithfully in a blaze of promises. We fell asleep under our striped umbrellas, the smell of the sea hot and alive in the salty air. Before we returned home, I walked a long length of beach, swinging a seaweed stem. The sky was blue and the call of gulls rang out in lively echoes. Small birds ran randomly to the waves and then away from them in an endless dance for food. It was all about survival. I carved a small heart and a larger one beside of it in the sand. The ocean rushed in and washed them out to sea.

Chapter Twenty-Eight

Katie and Mandy were running late, but finally we heard a large splutter and roar announcing their arrival. Mandy seemed to be herself, or some unhealthy quiet version of herself. She was in oversized overalls and a long sleeve shirt. Katie was upset.

"Can you believe that?" she said, pointing to a rusty, antique van parked at the curve. There seemed to be steam rising from the radiator.

"What is it?" Kat laughed. "Obviously not Billy Mac's best!"

"A fossilized representation of days gone by," Alba said.

"That," Katie said dramatically, "is what Billy Mac expects me to drive while my car is being repaired."

Somewhere, in the hillside of cars waiting for repairs, Katie's car longed for daylight and repairs, while Billy Mac cast his love spells her way.

"He asked me to marry him," Katie said. "I said no, in the nicest way possible, and this is what he gives me to drive."

"There's a roar in my head," Mandy said. "I cannot tolerate this sort of transportation."

"Then you can walk home," Katie said furiously. "I'll probably never be able to start it again, anyway."

I poured everyone coffee and we sat down at the round table.

"I have news," Darrie said. "Chuck and I are getting married."

"Has he finally found a job to his specifications?" Kat asked.

"Does he have a divorce?" Alba said.

"Don't forget birth control," Katie said wisely. "You don't want to end up with a baby that isn't his!"

"I'm starving," Mandy said, folding her arms on the table and resting her head on them.

"Don't be so negative," I said, feeling sorry for Darrie's confused look of wonderment. "Things could work out."

"That's true," Kat said. "Any moment the love fairy could tap him with her magic wand and turn him into a man."

"Kat," I said warningly, and then turned to Darrie.

"When is the big day," I asked cheerfully.

"Well," she said, "as soon as he gets a divorce, and a job, and proves those kids aren't his, we're renting the community center and throwing a big wedding."

"I want to be home in time to see who wins the beauty pageant," Mandy interrupted sullenly. She had a passion for pageants. Kat said if she ever won, she'd have to drag the bouquet of roses down the walkway, being of such a frail and chronically ill disposition.

"Forget that freaking pageant, Mandy!" Katie said. "We'll be lucky to even get home in that piece of junk."

"The girl down at floral shop is giving me a discount on arrangements," Darrie said.

"Does anyone smell lilacs?" Alba asked. "There's a heavy smell of lilacs here."

"I just hope his crazy wife doesn't try anything," Darrie said.

"Like having him arrested for bigamy," Kat murmured.

"My boyfriend was raped," Darrie said suddenly. "That's what happened. It was right after he got out of the navy. He was at the beach with some of his friends and a woman approached him and offered him a drink. He took her to his motel room to show her his navy photos. She put something in his drink. He was still conscious but could not move. She had her way with him, and stole his driver's license. A year later he was served with papers for child support. The judge refused to listen to his side of the story."

"C'mon," Kat said, "he's told that same story for all of his kids. No one can be raped that many times unless they're complete idiots. And why would he then marry her, anyway?"

"For the children," Darrie said uncertainly.

"Here," I said, "eat this." I handed Darrie two large brownies with nuts. She began eating quietly.

"Hey, girls," I said, "Mrs. Crank is having her party next Saturday. She wants all of you to attend. I know that you said you'd make the pineapple upside down cake for her, Alba, and she needs you to cater, Kat. It should be a lot of fun."

Everyone agreed to show up and we continued discussing the party, the wedding, the van, and date rape. Finally everyone said goodnight. I stayed up very late watching old movies and fell asleep to the sound of the television.

Chapter Twenty-Nine

"How are things going," Doc asked. He was sitting across from me, smiling. He seemed to be in a good mood and I didn't want to ruin it for him, so I said, "Fine!"

"Define fine," he said.

"I'm helping Mrs. Crank give a party at the home," I said. He nodded and waited patiently.

"You seem happy about it," he said finally. He said that because I was smiling nervously, I suppose, or maybe it was the comically high brows I still sported.

"Yes," I said. "She's been keeping us both busy. She has invited some old friends, plus my friends, and, of course, all the other residents."

"Very costly, I imagine," he said. "Very kind of her."

"She is a very kind person," I said.

"What about you? Are you having headaches, panic attacks?" he asked.

"Sometimes," I said.

For some reason, I felt quiet inside and tired. I didn't really feel like talking. He asked about the Friday night round table events and I told him the latest news with the girls.

"Are you concerned for Darrie," he asked. "Her refusal to accept the realities of her situation?"

"No," I said, "Reality never did a thing for Darrie. The fantasy and dreams she has for herself and Chuck seem to keep her happy and enthused. Her true reality is too lonely to deal with. She doesn't have to focus on herself if she can just focus on someone else, someone in worse shape than she is."

"What do you feel about that?"

"She might as well find happiness in dreams," I said.

"What do you think of Mandy's personalities?"

"We're all fragments," I said. "We have ours in one solid form; Mandy has pieces that come loose."

"That's an odd thing to say," he mused.

"Well," I shrugged, "it is one of the reasons I see you. Mandy lives in pieces, I see in pieces. I have no idea what the norm of things might be, or if it even exists. What perfect pattern can we hold up and say, 'See this, see how we should all be'? If I were shown such a thing, I'd think that somewhere, hidden, were threads unraveling in silence."

"I see," he said. We talked a while longer and I left for home. I still felt quiet inside, as though my body was holding its breath, waiting to exhale.

Chapter Thirty

"How should I use the Alabama Crystal," Kat asked. We were sitting at the round table, having coffee and half listening to Cat Stevens.

"I don't know," I said. "It has to be your choice."

"Well," Kat said, "it's just that I almost don't want to use it and pass it on to anyone else. I feel close to all of them while I hold it, Aunt El, Mother, our grandparents, the ancestors. We're the last of our direct line, so obviously it will have to be passed to a friend." Kat unzipped her vest to reveal the crystal. She said she had worn it against her heart from the first night that she received it. She said that sometimes she could sense its warmth and power flickering there. Just then, Alba knocked and came into the kitchen.

"Good morning," she said, "Do you want company or is this private?"

"No, it's okay," I said. "Kat and I are having coffee. Let me pour you a cup." I handed Alba her coffee, she took a sip and glanced over at Kat. Then she froze.

"Where did you get that necklace?" she asked.

"That's the Alabama Crystal," I said. "Remember I told you about it before."

"Yes," she said, "but you told me that it was lost when your Aunt El died."

"So it was," I said. "But I received a mysterious package by mail addressed in Aunt El's handwriting, and the crystal was inside. I don't have any answers. I only know that it arrived and that it's Kat's turn to use it."

"Have you used it," Alba asked.

"No, not yet," Kat said. She took the necklace off and held it to the light.

"Look at this," she said. "It's beautiful in the light."

The crystal turned from hard glare to soft glow as the light struck it. It seemed alive in Kat's hand.

"It is beautiful," Alba said in a strangled voice. For a moment, I feared she'd swallowed her coffee down the wrong pipes. Then she gave a tight lipped smile. She looked ready to cry.

"What's wrong," I asked.

"Nothing," she said. "I just think that it is very beautiful. I can't believe you're wearing it. Aren't you afraid of losing it?"

"No," Kat said, "somehow I get the feeling that I can't lose it. It feels alive, as if it knows that I have to use it before it can be passed on. I know that sounds weird, but that's the feeling it gives me."

"It doesn't sound weird to me at all," Alba said. She drank her coffee as we discussed the crystal. Her eyes kept drifting back to it. She seemed quieter than usual, and when Kat left, she said she had some things to do and left behind her.

I was happy that Kat had the crystal and for the connection it gave her to our mother and Aunt El. I hoped that when she did use it she'd use it for something wonderful. I also hoped I'd be there to witness it. The crystal made a difference in my life. Somehow I felt safe and Kat was safe as long as the crystal was safe. For it to return after so many years had to be a good omen. There had to an explanation and I felt sure it would be revealed. For the moment, I felt as though Aunt El was still looking out for our welfare.

Chapter Thirty-One

Mrs. Crank was up early and in full command when I arrived at the home. She was giving orders for the decoration of the dining hall. To insure the good graces of the nursing staff, which she hoped to keep from attending, she had ordered a free bar and lots of appetizers to be set up in the nurses lounge. She asked if I had used the bow and arrows. I told her that Kat was making a target for me, and that I planned to use it soon. She smiled and nodded, then returned to her preparations. When she was ready for lunch, we settled at a small table in the dining hall.

I told her about the Alabama Crystal and how much Kat loved it. I explained about its glow, and how Kat held it up to the light for Alba to admire. "It seems alive sometimes," I said.

"So Alba admires the crystal," she asked.

"Oh, yes. I told her about it about a year ago, and she said it was a shame that it was lost so long. She was thrilled to finally see it. She said it reminded her of a quest. She looked as though she might cry. Alba is so dramatic at times, then, at other times, she's impossible to get any emotion out of whatsoever."

"Did you tell all the girls that I wanted them to attend the party?" she asked.

"Yes," I said, "and everyone seems to be looking forward to it. I know I am. Do you remember telling me you'd teach me to swing dance?"

She laughed." I fear that I might break some vital limb," she said, "so I've arranged for you a partner. I have also arranged a partner for myself, an old friend, but I doubt that we will swing so much as glide across the dance floor."

"I can't wait to see it," I said, giving her a hug. When I left, she told me to use the bow, and I promised to do so.

I think her two children missed a great deal in not knowing their mother very well. Mrs. Crank often said that they took after their father, a stoic, practical man with no room in his life for fantasy. "I'm afraid I took him on a merry chase," she would sigh. Sometimes she appeared so full of life, and at others, quite frail and vulnerable. Sometimes, looking around the home, I felt overwhelmed at the loneliness of some of the residents. They would wait day after day for letters that would never arrive, watch the windows for faces that did not appear. It was a sad life for most of them.

When I was small I asked Aunt El if she would purchase a bow and arrow set for me for Christmas.

"Whatever for?" she had exclaimed.

I tried to explain how much I enjoyed them. Watching cowboy movies, my fascination lay with the quiver and arrows, each decorated carefully and colorfully, used by the Indians. The bows seemed so graceful and smooth.

She said they were expensive and dangerous, so I never asked again. Perhaps it was the Alabama Crystal and the story of the shaman that fueled her reaction. I could picture him in his village among the braves and the women and the bows. I had read that the bows cut in one long piece of hickory were best. I was pleased that the one I now owned wore the mark of an excellent bow maker out west. Kat brought the target over when I called her and settled back to watch. At first my aim was terrible. I would pull back a little at a time until my hand shook. Finally I realized that I had to pull back in one fluid motion to achieve any sort of good result. If I hesitated while pulling, it was too difficult to continue. Eventually I hit the bull's eye and Kat shouted, "Bravo!" She took a few tries at it before she left, but shook her head and said it seemed pointless to her, but added she was pleased that I enjoyed it. After she left, Alba, who had been watching from her back porch, came over to investigate. She was in one of her neat pale blue suits, so I was surprised when she asked if she could shoot. She held the bow and studied it from end to end. She investigated the ties and the brand name, then she nodded, as though satisfied, and let fly an arrow. She hit the bull's eye straight off.

I was astonished and put it down to luck, but she pulled all six arrows and hit straight on each time.

"Alba," I said, "how did you do that?"

"I took archery in college," she said. "I wasn't into any of the sports, but we were required to take something."

"You're a natural," I said.

"This is a beautiful piece of work," she said. "Actually, the best money can buy."

I agreed and explained that Mrs. Crank had ordered it for me as a gift.

"I'll help you with it if you like," she said. "It's excellent exercise for the arms and also for the mind."

That seemed true enough. I could feel my arms starting to ache a bit, which meant I had used muscles that seldom had a chance to work out. Also, there was something peaceful and beautiful in the fluid movement of the arrow and the satisfying hit of the target.

"You're welcome to shoot with me any time," I said.

***

It was dark outside and raining. I was having a terrible time trying to sleep. The clock announced that it was twelve midnight. The walls seemed smaller, and I could feel my nerves edging toward anxiety.

I got up and drank some chocolate milk. I put the laundry in the washer, and swept and mopped the kitchen. The phone rang. I was surprised because it was late, and also a little worried that an accident had occurred with someone I loved.

"Hey," Kat said, "It's me. Katie and I just drove by and saw your light on. In fact, the whole house is lit up like Christmas Eve. Everything okay?"

"No," I said. "I feel so anxious, and for no reason, just restless."

"Wanna sing?" she asked "We have the mics and the karaoke machine with us."

"Sure," I said. "Come on back." I love to sing. I especially love to sing happy songs to blue panic and ornery anxiety.

Chapter Thirty-Two

Kat and Katie set everything up in the living room. They'd been singing all evening, but were always happy to show their ability. They were really amazingly good. They had perfect pitch, and had sung together for years. I sang *It's a Wonderful World* as a warm up and then plunged into *The Night They Drove Old Dixie Down*. I brought out the potato chips and dip, and some veggies for righteousness' sake. We all sang some Neil Young songs together. Before I knew it, the clock was striking four.

"You okay now?" Kat asked.

I said, "Yes, thank you, Kat," and hugged both of them goodbye. The shadows in my room had escaped with the sound of music, just as I had known they would. I was ready to jump into bed when the phone rang again. It was Mandy. She had woken and found Katie still out at karaoke.

"I'm scared," she said. "Do you like me, Sylvie?"

"Yes," I said, "very much." It was true. Her personalities could be annoying, or cruel, or funny, but the sad, underlying little girl was always there. Mandy's childhood had been taken by the preacher. She was too shattered to ever reclaim it.

"Don't worry, Mandy," I said. "The girls stopped by here to sing a few songs, but they're on the way home now. They should be there anytime."

"Why did they stop there?" she asked.

"I was on the verge of panic and up pacing around. They saw that all my lights were still on."

"Were you afraid?" she asked.

"Yes," I said, "but I was trying very hard not to be."

"Ya shoulda called me," a tough voice said. "I protect people."

"Thank you," I said. "Will you protect Mandy? Kat will be there soon."

"Okay," the voice said. "Call if ya need me."

"I will," I said. "Goodnight."

"Night," the voice said, and I hung up the phone.

I was going to lie down when I heard noises next door. It was Alba, apparently having a party for one. She had the grill on her back porch blazing. I walked over to investigate. Alba is a creature of habit. She is not in the habit of grilling in the middle of the night.

"What are you doing?".

"What do you care?" she said "You never listen to anything I say." She is not in the habit of snapping my head off either, so I persisted. "What's going on," I asked. "It smells like you're burning weeds. You aren't a secret marijuana farmer, are you?" No sign of a smile, she just continued with the fire, adding small leaves from a bag in her left hand.

"This is nothing to laugh at," she said. "These herbs are more powerful than you know."

"Well, okay, maybe, but why are you burning them?"

"The spirits have spoken to me. A great event will soon occur which will change many lives," she said.

"A natural occurrence," I asked.

"You could say that," she said. "It is not all unnatural. There is an event that will occur and it will affect our lives. I'm adding different herbs to ensure that it will not affect them negatively."

"Alba, you are such a puzzle sometimes," I said. "Do you want me to sit up with you?"

"It doesn't matter," she said. "I'm used to being alone a great deal."

"Yes," I replied, "but not in the middle of the night over an open flame." I thought it best to stick around in case Alba was having some sort of menopausal experience that the women's health almanac had failed to mention. She talked for a long time, and explained to me that she had been trained as a child to use the natural forces of the earth to deal with problems.

"What problem is it?" I asked, point blank.

"It's more of a miracle." she said mysteriously, and then hugged me. It certainly seemed like a miracle. Alba was pretty stingy in the hugging department.

"It is kinda pretty out here," I said, "you know, in that dark, spooky, dramatic sort of way."

She laughed. "The night is always alive in its silence. It is the spirit of emotions that have gone before us. The essence of everything lingers. It's like the Alabama Crystal that you are so fond of. Ancestors cling in tiny parts, each spirit adding something to it."

"That makes it sound so otherworldly," I said. "It is a beautiful and unusual rock, though."

"You don't have to stay out here with me," she said. "I'm okay."

"Oh, I love the outdoors," I said. Actually, I was uneasy that she was on the verge of some sort of breakdown. Always standing a little too near one myself, I understood how the night could bring pain and despair. She looked at me and smiled. "Well," she said, "I'm all out of herbs. I guess we can return to our beds."

"Do you think the herbs worked," I asked. "Did whatever they were supposed to do?"

"Yes," she said, "and your arrival here to stand with me only proves it."

"What do you mean?"

"Nothing," she said. "Try to get some sleep. Thank you for standing beside me."

"I'm incurably nosy," I said, and laughed. "I'll see you tomorrow."

"Goodnight," she said, and disappeared into her house.

It's my fine and edgy opinion that we're on part of a great woven rug of sky. That we meet again and again to work and play out certain situations and dreams. Sometimes I felt as if I had always known Alba, Darrie, Katie, and Mandy. They were so important in the lives that Kat and I had made after the loss of Aunt El. It felt right that we all shared each other's worlds. I walked slowly across the lawn home. I felt very sleepy suddenly. It had been a strange night. The lights were already off at Alba's. I wasn't sure what her ceremony was for, but I had faith that she'd performed it with the best of intentions. When I entered my house, it suddenly seemed I could smell lilacs. I imagine Alba's constant suggestion was the cause. It was not an unpleasant smell at all. I slipped under the covers quietly and fell asleep.

Chapter Thirty-Three

Sunday morning peered through the window without an invitation, throwing her yellow eyes brightly around the room. I sat up and blinked, afraid that I had overslept. Then I remembered that Mrs. Crank did not need me today. She was spending the day with a friend. My sensory cells were still sleeping, but my eyes were squinting against the sunlight. I had only pulled my robe together and was fumbling for a tie when Kat and Katie called, both of them enthused with a new idea. They said they'd be over in about fifteen minutes. I made coffee and set out some donuts. I pulled the blinds high at the kitchen window, and my eyes recoiled sullenly, but I persisted in my self-inflicted punishment, and opened the back door, too. I heard Kat and Katie pull up outside. The muffler had fallen off the old van that Katie was still driving, at least until she could be more positive on the marriage question from Billy Mac. Actually, most of the neighborhood could hear them pull up. Of course, as a whole, the neighborhood was used to Sunday morning noise, as we sported several very elderly residents who blasted their televisions at full volume in order to hear Sunday Morning Preaching Hour. Katie was wearing her long hippie dress and pink inspiration cowboy boots. She always wore them to find new ideas or to follow one of Kat's. Kat was in her usual jeans and cotton shirt. They came in and grabbed coffee cups and donuts, then sat down, leaning forward in their seats in excitement.

"You look like you just woke up!" Katie said.

Kat ignored the obvious and said, "Sylvie, we have an excellent idea. I know it will be profitable!"

"Okay, now, be honest, and tell us what you think of this. We have decided to add on to my catering business. I've been writing songs for a while now, so the plan is to make up some cards that say 'Sing and Serve'! We plan to leave them around town and hope that people pick up on it. Some of my better customers are already interested."

"What does sing and serve mean?" I asked.

"Just what it says," she replied. "We go in and set up, we sing for the dinner guests and then we retire to the kitchen to cater the meal. What do you think? I had a CD made with the music to the songs I've written."

She put the CD in. She and Kat began to sing. It was a nostalgic piece, full of broken hearts and promises. It was an exceptional performance.

"Wow, Kat, I love the words. It's a beautiful song."

"Thanks," she grinned. "Now let us perform this masterpiece for you once more!"

They sang and the music was soft. The words flowed in a swan song of longing, unrequited love, and remembrance.

Kat sang the first verse, and Katie the second. On the chorus, Kat's deeper voice punctuated sadness, as Katie crooned in her higher, sweet tone. The whole thing was put together very well. I was impressed and said so. I also loved the name. Sing and Serve was a perfect logo.

"You really like it?" Kat said anxiously. I assured her that I did. Kat said she had a notebook of songs and hoped to have CDs made of the music.

"It's either that or learn to play the guitar," she said, "and I'm a little tight on time."

"I have an idea," I said. "Why don't you try out your new idea at Mrs. Crank's party? I'm sure she'd love it. She has lots of influential friends coming, and they might book you."

"Yeah!" Katie squealed. "That would be perfect!"

"Yes, it really would be," Kat said thoughtfully. "Thanks. You're the best."

"Takes one to know one," I said. An old line we used to tease each other with.

"I even like it," Alba said.

We all jumped and looked around. Alba had let herself in and stood smiling,

"I heard the entire song, but didn't want to interrupt," she said. "It really is an excellent sound and the words are catchy. They linger in your head, which is what one should look for in a song."

"Thanks, Alba," Kat said. "I know that's high praise coming from you."

I poured coffee for Alba and we all sat down at the table. We talked at length about various people in town that might be interested in the Sing and Serve idea. I was very proud of Kat and Katie. I knew that Mrs. Crank would like the idea. I was also pleased that Alba was so supportive. She seemed genuinely impressed and pleased with them.

After everyone left, I felt the blue of loneliness. I had attended church throughout my childhood, and suddenly I longed to be sitting somewhere in a pew, absorbing the atmosphere. Throughout my life, in troubled times, I had entered random churches and sat quietly, listening and thinking. I decided to attend the Lee Street Baptist. I arrived at the church in time to follow the preacher in. He turned to see who was following, and smiled and shook my hand in a welcome.

The sermon and prayer waned quiet and dignified. I relaxed into the tranquility of colors bursting through the stained glass windows. There seemed to be a large number of people in attendance, possibly spiked by the low economy. People seem to need faith most when the money's gone.

When I was a child, church was the mainspring of our town, of most small towns. It was the social center. A meeting house that could be used literally to meet new people. Singers and young ministers from other areas were often invited to preach or sing. The minister announced that he had special guest singers. The day itself was a song with the golden sun and distant wild birdcalls. A large lady heaved herself to the front followed by two rail thin young girls. The woman wore a red dress and the two young girls wore pink.

It was a bluesy trio. The woman came alive on the microphone and moved back and forth with the grace of a sailboat in full wind. The girls darted and danced behind, shouting Oh, yes! Amen! and Oooooooooooooooh! at appropriate places. It was invigorating and lively. They did five songs and the congregation applauded happily. The woman had a pure voice that conveyed emotion so well. The minister announced that it was homecoming day and for any guests to join them directly after church. With Kat and Alba as the main competing cooks in my life, I knew I would decline the invitation.

Everyone seemed to leave the church feeling very alive. I know I did. I walked out into the sunshine and smiled. I stopped to watch the women lay out the homecoming food. Macaroni salad, potato salad, rolls, roast, cornbread, steaming pots of corn on the cob, and a large selection of cake and pies. I thought of how much food there was here and how little in so many other places, not just around the world, but in our own country. I wondered what a huge difference it might make if all the church homecomings, all over our land, invited their own local homeless singles and families to attend the meal. If such a plan was assigned to my hands, I'd put out notices to alert the homeless. They wouldn't be forced to attend the services, because it would be wrong to shove religion down an unwilling throat, but simply to drop by to eat. Suddenly, I realized that I should speed up. Mrs. Crank had a list for me. I waved a last goodbye to the minister.

Chapter Thirty-Four

It is Wednesday and I am talking to Doc.

"Do you think I'm manic depressive, Doc?"

"No," he said.

"Then what sort of label do you have written down in your book for me?" I was curious and wondered what he'd say. I was also wondering if I could conform to any label he might render.

"I think it's best not to label people, Sylvia," he said.

"But I thought that it was your job to," I persisted. "I might feel more secure with a label. I could study it and find ways to correct it."

He laughed, "Hmmm, we could say you have acute anxiety."

"That's not very exotic," I said. "Everyone has anxiety to some degree."

"That's true," he said, "which is why I see no need to label it."

"Aunt El used to say, 'Never call a person something they cannot help being'. It was like, never call a person what they are."

"What do you mean," he asked.

"Well, never call a blind person blind, or an ugly person ugly."

"Why do you think she said that," he asked.

"I don't know. I assume she meant if you cannot help a person, if you cannot change their condition, and if they cannot change it, it is useless to speak of it, possibly even cruel to speak of it."

"In some cases that may be true," he said, "but in your case, we may speak of it, because It's something that can be helped and changed."

"Anxiety is quick, like a thief at a stop light, jumping in unexpectedly. Suddenly you're sweating, shaking, your heart is racing, and Anxiety just sits there, dangerous and vicious. You know he has a weapon and isn't afraid to use it." I sat back.

"I'm trying to teach you to lock your doors," he said.

"I keep forgetting," I said. "And I resent locking them, anyway. Why can't I just ride free, the wind in my hair, calm and peaceful. The act of locking my doors creates anxiety in itself. It's acknowledging that something is out there. I'm locking something out."

"You're taking control," he said. "We all have to acknowledge that there is something out there. We have to set boundaries to protect ourselves."

"I guess I just want us all to live in peace and harmony. I want us to all love each other," I said.

"It's a wonderful sentiment," he said, "and idealistic, but it didn't work in the seventies, and it won't work now. There are many, many wonderful people in the world. But think of ying and yang. There is a balance of bad also. If we don't protect ourselves, it's likely no one will. I want you to set boundaries so that you're not taken advantage of. It's the same as teaching a small child not to play in the street. If the child isn't taught boundaries, he's put into a dangerous situation."

Suddenly, I wanted to be outdoors. I wanted to feel the sun and look up into the endless blue of the sky. I felt constricted in my chair, as though a thousand words were spilling on the floor around my feet. I was tired of choosing which ones to step on and which ones to avoid.

"I need to go now." I said.

I left hurriedly. I did not have a sudden dawning and understanding, I did not want to take out the pieces of my life. I wanted things in small compartments of my brain, where I could leave them to look through in understanding and at my own leisure. There was no chance of looking into endless blue skies, either. Rain fell in a steady gray sheet and I jumped into my car cold and wet. I sat there with the rain a curtain canopy around the windows. I couldn't see out and no one could see in. The steady beat of water on the windows lulled me. I put my seat back and stared out. I turned the heater on and the warmth made me sleepy and tired.

Finally I started the car and went home. I didn't care about the rain. I took my bow and arrow and shot, over and over, into the yellow and red of the target circles. If some of the water running down my face was warm, it made no difference. I was furious at the target. The bull's eye glowed angrily back at me. I kept missing it with the arrows, over and over again.

Chapter Thirty-Five

The Sing and Serve business was booming. Mrs. Crank had gently lead her friends into believing that Kat and Katie should be a staple at every party. Hers hadn't occurred yet, but she was still loyally advertising Kat and Katie's skills.

Katie had music CDs made of all the songs that Kat had written. She organized the singing schedules, while Kat cooked like a mad woman. They appointed Mandy dishwasher and gave her a hefty allowance. She was pleased to be making her own money. They wanted her to help serve, but decided against it. She was too slow and, when frightened, would escape into whatever personality surfaced first. Everything was going very well until the Mama, Irene, decided to come and force Mandy to return to Florida with her.

Naturally she arrived on a Friday night as we were happily discussing the profits from Sing and Serve. Alba was impressed and anxious to hear what foods were being offered. Darrie was impressed, too, as much as she could be in her love-induced fog. In the midst of the laughter, someone rang the doorbell. I opened it to find Irene and John, Katie's parents, on the welcome mat. Irene was glowering. John just grinned.

"Where are my daughters," she asked, stepping around me and heading toward the sound of laughter. As I shut the door, I could tell from the dead silence that she had found them.

After a hesitation, I heard Katie say, "Mama, what are you doing here?"

John lagged into the shadows as far as he could. I could see that Mandy was shrinking rapidly inside her huge sweater. Katie, an optimist to the end, tried to hug her mother, but Mama was having none of it.

"Mandy," she said, "we were forced, because of your foolishness, to drive all the way up here. We're taking you home."

"No, thank you," Mandy said, as vaguely as if she had been offered a tissue.

"No, thank you?" Mama said, putting emphasis on each word, "Do you really think that I have gone to all this trouble for a 'no, thank you?'" Mandy didn't say a word.

"She doesn't want to go back, Mama," Katie said. "She even has a job now. Why don't you and Daddy spend the night with us? We have some great food already prepared at the house."

Mama continued to stare at Mandy. "Mandy," she said in a sad voice, "you have broken my heart. I have fought chest pains through three states, just to see my baby, just to take my baby home."

"It's true, baby," John said. "Mama is sick." Mandy remained seated.

"Get up and get in the car!" Mama suddenly shrieked. Mandy and Katie jumped.

"Please don't scream at them that way," Kat said.

Mama whirled to redirect her rage. She bulged with rage. "How dare you interfere when I am speaking to my children," she said. "Why, you're a woman lover, a lover of your own kind and doomed to hell. I am sick of your evil influences over my children."

Then she turned to me, "And you, I will call down curses upon your household. What kind of church do you attend? Which one allows you all to party and cavort, and act as though life is a game?"

"Mama," Katie said, "Please, Mama, Mandy and I are happy here. Home holds bad memories for Mandy. She needs to stay here. She's making her own money, and we have a good life. We are happy, Mama. Please come home with us now. We can talk about things."

Mama suddenly grabbed Mandy and jerked her to her feet. Mandy went limp and fell to escape her grip. She curled into a fetal position.

"Carry her on out, John," Mama said.

"You are not carrying her out," I said. "I want you to leave this house now." She tried to lift Mandy by her long hair. Several strands came out in her hands.

"I will call the police," Mama said.

"Mandy is old enough to make her own decisions," I said, "and she's decided to stay."

On the floor Mandy covered her ears with her hands and squeezed her eyes shut. Katie was biting her fingernails and staring toward her father.

"Get out," I said.

John drifted over and tugged at Irene's arm. "Come on, Mama," he said.

She elbowed away from him and glared at me with contempt.

"You," she said, "what kind of a Christian are you?"

I leaned in close so that Mandy and the others could not hear.

"I'm not sure, I said, "but I am sure that I'm not the kind to prostitute little girls out for cash, to steal childhoods, or lock the door on my own daughter out of envy for her youth and beauty. I am not the kind that viciously controls the movements of anyone that tries to love me, nor do I enter other people's homes rudely when my sense of cruel control is threatened. I guess I'm the kind that refuses to cast pearls before swine, and if you do not leave now, I may be the kind that kicks your ass all the way out to the curb."

After they drove away, there was a long silence.

"Well," Alba said, "that was very unpleasant. Now, Kat, what about that cake you were telling me about? Did you use both the yellow and white of the egg or just the white?"

"Just the white," Kat said slowly, then smiled at Alba, and began spouting off a long list of ingredients.

Darrie pulled Mandy from the floor and asked her what the kitchens looked like in the houses they had worked in so far. Mandy slowly began describing the kitchens. Her face seemed to glow with purpose. She described different cleaning utensils and her special ability to do the job. She said her job was easy and that she was going to save her money for a dress for Mrs. Crank's party.

Katie was smiling and watching Mandy's face. By now, Mandy should have performed a personality change, but she was holding her own. For the moment, she had the confidence to be herself. She had the support to stand on her own. She had fallen into the fetal position, but she had not stayed there.

Chapter Thirty-Six

I dread confrontations and go to great lengths to avoid them. Since I was unable to avoid a confrontation with Katie and Mandy's parents, I knew that panic was already grinning in the wings. I tried doing yard work, since physical activity was supposed to help. I threw exaggerated effort into my movements. Sometimes it was possible to convince myself that I was too busy to be scared. That was not the case today. Already an insidious group of thoughts were stealthily entering my airways. My mind was being consumed with a dread of death. The dread of death lay in the fact that I was losing the ability to breathe. This forced me to try for deep breaths. When I could not breathe deeply, I became even more fearful. On the outside, I knew that I appeared to be a simple woman calmly cleaning her yard. On the inside, my mind raced with thoughts of gloom and doom. I would have to accept that I was destined to die alone, while looking perfectly normal. I dropped the rake and hurried into the kitchen, not even stopping to lock the door. All I cared about were the keys and ignition. Then I was on the road. At first I drove fast, then, as I neared the hospital, I dropped to a reasonable speed. I parked and admired the view. I kept the window down in case someone stumbled upon my body later and needed to unlock the car door to get me out. I felt safe here, as I supposed that, with my last breath, I might have the ability to roll from the car, thereby saving someone the trouble of opening the door after all. After a lengthy time, I wanted to go home, but it wasn't possible to return there immediately. I drove through several parking lots and stopped at a fast food joint for coffee. I read somewhere once that coffee helps improve breathing.

Finally, the Xanax I had taken at the hospital kicked in and I grew calm. I also grew very exhausted. I drove home and fell asleep on the couch. When I woke up Kat was sitting cross legged on a large floor pillow.

"Hi," I said. "I didn't hear you come in."

"Yeah, you were really snoozing," she said. "Putting in more time at the hospital parking lot? I thought I saw you leaving there earlier."

"I'm okay now," I said. Kat is very protective. I knew she was concerned. "I'm sorry if I caused you to worry.".

"You care too much," she said. "You should learn to let things flow through your hands. Picture everything that bothers you moving through your fingertips and on out the door. And the doc is right; you should get out more, date someone, for God's sake!"

"Advice that you might take yourself," I said.

"Look," she said, "I'm content the way I am. If I had been a man, I would probably have chosen the monastery. The only passion I feel at this point in my life is a passion for my music.

"I have a passion for reading," I pointed out.

"You have a passion for everything," she said, "which is why you should find someone. You could have a family."

"I do have a family," I said. "I guess we're alike. I enjoy things the way they are. By the way, how are things going with the new song you're working on?"

"Which one?" she said. "I have about four near completion. I'm looking forward to singing at Mrs. Crank's party. Katie's pretty excited about it, too."

"That sounds great," I said.

"Mandy said that Katie and I were her favorite singers."

"You have really worked wonders with her, Kat."

"She loves being independent. We haven't had a personality emerge in a week, which is a great score for her. Anyway, I just dropped by for a minute. I have some writing to do."

"Kat, thank you for coming here and caring and sitting with me," I said.

"You snore." she said with a big grin, then hugged me and left.

I felt more rested now, and decided to take a bath. We had a variety of oils, fizz soaps, and bath pearls on hand. I added a little of everything to the water. I lit candles and placed three on the side of the tub and two on the sink. With the blinds drawn and the lights off, the candles created a peaceful feel of seclusion as the broad assortment of scents mingled with the bath bubbles. I climbed in the hot water and lay my head back against the bath pillow. All of my exhaustion was draining away in the water. What the bit of sleep had not restored was now renewed by the bath.

I felt more energetic, and, as always after a battle of severe stress, grateful that the memory of it was disappearing even as I slid the French milled soap across my body. I wanted time to think about the Alabama Crystal. After Kat, where could the crystal go but to a friend, since no bloodlines existed? We were without relatives. I didn't want to dwell on the crystal, but I understood how Kat could be uncertain. I didn't want to doubt, but the crystal seemed to have a will and purpose apart from us. Aunt El had said once that no matter how the crystal was valued in the family, the fact remained that it had originally been stolen. She said that since the shaman had given the crystal and his word while intoxicated, he had been unable to retract either without a loss of face. I realized that thinking of it was breaking the harmony I had gained through the bath. I got dressed and decided to ride into town for a few things and then visit Mrs. Crank.

Chapter Thirty-Seven

Mrs. Crank asked for a CD of Kat's song. She wanted the band she hired to play it at the party while Katie and Kat sang. In fact, I was on my way to meet the girls. I had picked up a few things at the store but now we were meeting for some serious shopping. We planned to cruise some favorite retail stores and later, meet for lunch at Diretti's. He was well known for his spaghetti and homemade bread.

Katie and Kat chose pale peach chiffon dresses, Alba decided on a dark brown silk dress, Mandy, a yellow shift, and I was captivated by a plain, white linen with a short jacket. We arrived at Diretti's starving. He brought out the spaghetti himself. The bread was a crispy, with creamy butter and warm brown garlic on top and a delicious blend of cheeses cooked inside. Diretti lingered to chat and to listen to our raves of pleasure regarding the food, and the talents of the chef. It was clear that his gruff mumblings were designed to hide a vulnerable nature and desire to please. I got the sense it wasn't easy for him to find the sort of appreciation he craved. Kat wore the crystal. She had developed a habit of touching it when she talked. Sing and Serve was attracting customers rapidly. After lunch, Katie and Mandy left for the Cut It Cute with Darrie. Both needed a shampoo and trim. Alba had to hurry home.

"I've used the crystal," Kat said, the moment everyone had disappeared.

"How did you use it," I asked.

"I wished for Katie and I to be successful with the business. I asked for financial security. I can't believe how well things are going, Sylvia. It's a dream come true. It makes me believe in the magic of the crystal. It was eerie the way it glowed. I felt an odd sense of warmth, as though it had begun to work immediately. Do you think I was just imagining things?"

"No," I said, "I felt the same warmth once."

"And it seemed to glow for you also?"

I nodded. I remembered the feeling long ago when I returned to the house to find our lives restored to order after the fire.

"That's wonderful," I said. "Let's celebrate." I hugged Kat and we waved down Diretti for two shrimp cocktails. We talked about the ancestor and the past and Aunt El.

"It seems so old fashioned to believe in a crystal," Kat said, "but it doesn't seem to be just a rock. There is truly something in it that illuminates and acknowledges the person carrying it. Do you want the crystal back now?"

"No," I said. "It's up to you now to pass it on."

"I guess so," she said.

"Just take your time, Kat, You'll know what to do when the time comes."

"I hope so," Kat said.

When Kat left, I rode home. The store bags lay in the seat beside of me. I felt a growing sense of excitement for the party. It would be fun to dress elegantly for once. I was even looking forward to the swing dance, although I was pretty sure that Mrs. Crank had lined up a partner who was quite a bit older. With Kat feeling so certain about her business, and a party to attend, I was in a peaceful mood. I arrived home to the sound of water dripping fast and loud in the bathroom. My skills were limited, but Kat had a knack for fixing things. I called and left a message on her phone. She had not returned home yet.

Chapter Thirty-Eight

Kat came over to look at a stripped pipe under the sink. From the kitchen I could hear her exclamations and curses. She was a wonderful fix-it gal, but the job was a tricky one. Her frustration was not helped by the fact that Darrie had arrived and perched on the shut toilet seat, asking for advice about Chuck.

Kat did not necessarily dislike men, but she did dislike Chuck. She said that he didn't qualify for the man category.

"It's not that I mind being the only one working," Darrie said. "It's just that it doesn't give us much opportunity to go out and do anything."

"Hmm," Kat said.

"And it really put us back when he lost the rent money. He thought it was somewhere in his car, but we've practically stripped the car and found nothing! I know he feels bad about it, and I've reassured him that it could happen to anybody, but it was really hard to make the rent again. Do you know what I mean?"

"Unfortunately," Kat said.

"What do you think? Do you think he's depressed because he wants to do more for me and isn't able to?"

"I don't know," Kat said. "My wish right now is to have a canvas and oils. Then I could paint you a picture."

"A picture of what," Darrie said in amazement. "I didn't know you could paint."

"Never mind," Kat said. "Would you hand me the pliers?"

"Yeah, here," Darrie said. "Anyway I have to get to work, Kat. Do you know if Katie has a way to the shop today? I'm supposed to do a shampoo for her."

"I can't say one way or the other," Kat said. "When I talked to her earlier, she was on her way to Billy Mac's to wrestle another car out of him. You could probably reach her there."

"Thanks, Kat," Darrie said. "Bye."

After Darrie left, I walked into the bathroom to see if Kat needed any help.

"No," she said, "it's getting there, just taking a little time."

"Thanks for fixing it, Kat," I said.

"No problem," she replied.

"Kat, have you noticed that none of us have a real relationship?"

"It has crossed my mind."

"Why do you think that is?"

"We're all crazy women,"

"I was trying to be serious," I said.

"We're all okay," Kat said. "This is just real life. There's not always a happy ending in real life. We do all right, and if we're meant to meet someone special someday, I'm sure we will, each one of us."

"Everything seems so hard and haphazard sometimes," I said, "I was hoping life would be prettier than this. What about the Alabama Crystal? Do you think it works? Do you see that it's made a difference in our lives?"

"I see that I am never going to get this done with all the yakking here," she said with a grin.

"Okay, okay, I'm leaving," I said, "I love you, Kat."

"I love you, too," she said.

Chapter Thirty-Nine

The night of the party was clear, with a full moon hanging over the parking lot. We unloaded Kat and Alba's food from Katie's van in an endless line of wonderful smells. Mrs. Crank was bright-eyed and excited. She met us in the kitchen. Her hair was pulled back in a thick, elegant bun. She wore a lavender dress that enhanced her lovely, fair complexion. She exclaimed over all the delicious dishes, especially Alba's cake.

True to their word, the nurses remained out of sight with their own buffet. It was nice, however, to know they were nearby in case of emergency. The girls were all beautiful in their new dresses. Alba said she smelled lilacs. I laughed and threw the door open to the party, where lilacs abounded. It was Mrs. Crank's choice of flowers for the night. "Well," Alba said, "at least tonight you have to admit that you smell lilacs, too."

Mrs. Crank's guests from the home had been seated by the nurses before they retired to their lounge. Her friends from town arrived fashionably late and were greeted by the doorman. The doorman's usual occupation was gardener, but tonight Mrs. Crank had urged him into a dark suit and tie.

The musicians were setting up on the stage that Mrs. Crank had ordered assembled. It was a slightly raised platform draped with a gray rug. Kat was conferring with them about her song. Katie was flirting with the bass player. Mandy was in the kitchen with Alba, who had taken her under her wing, and with Darrie. Darrie was waiting for her date at the back door. We were all surprised when a beat-up Oldsmobile pulled in with various ages of children swinging out the windows. It sounded like a small school bus. A tired-looking woman made her way to the back door. She kept turning to threaten the children in the car, warning them to stay seated. She walked straight up to Darrie.

"Hey," she said, "Chuck sent me to tell you that he can't make it. He's back in jail for breaking probation."

"What do you mean?" Darrie asked. "How do you know? He was at home getting dressed when I left."

"He called me from the jail. He was on his way here when he was picked up for possession. I think he may be going away for a while," the woman continued. "This is his fifth offense." Darrie stood staring at the woman. "Why did you come here?"

"I felt sorry for you, you know, waiting here and not knowing." Suddenly Darrie's eyes filled with compassion and understanding.

"I am sorry," Darrie said. "I have made a terrible mistake with your husband."

"That's okay," the woman said dully, "so did I. The difference is, I don't think I can fix my mistakes any time soon, but I think that you can."

"Thank you for coming here," Darrie said. "Tell Chuck that he won't be seeing me again. I'm sorry for any grief I caused you and the children." The woman nodded and walked back to her car. The children waved goodbye as she drove away. We were at a loss of words to comfort Darrie, but she appeared to be composed. Sometimes it is best to say nothing, which was what we did. Mrs. Crank called everyone in to be seated and announced that Kat and Katie would be performing the first song.

When they begin to sing, the place was quiet and the words drifted poignantly into the crowd. It was a beautiful song of love gone wrong, and one we could all identify with. They ended to tremendous applause. The band took over from there and everyone who was ambulatory stood up to dance.

From time to time throughout the night I could see Mrs. Crank and Alba huddled in conversation. I was glad that the two of them seemed to have a natural liking for each other. All the girls were dancing with the residents and guests. An elderly man was teaching me to swing dance. He was very agile for his age, and had a great enthusiasm for dancing. By the end of the evening I felt like a ragdoll, having been tossed and turned constantly. We all had a wonderful time, and I was pleased to see Mrs. Crank dancing and laughing. The party seemed to be everything that she'd hoped it would be. At midnight, the nurses appeared and began escorting people back to their rooms. When the place was empty, I walked with Mrs. Crank back to hers.

"I had a wonderful time," she said. "Do you think everyone enjoyed themselves?"

"It was an excellent party," I said. "I think you can say you're a big success as a party woman!"

She laughed, "Thank you, but now all I can think of is bed."

I hugged her goodnight and hurried to help the girls clean up and pack their things. Everyone seemed happy, but exhausted. I knew no one would have trouble sleeping. Not even Darrie, for although it was a blow to her, I think she finally understood the situation with Chuck.

Chapter Forty

On Monday I decided to go through the photo albums that Kat and I had carried with us for years, finally storing them in my extra bedroom until we had time to sort through them. I called Kat to help divide up the pictures. I wanted each of us to choose the photos we wanted to keep personally. I bought several scrapbooks. When Kat arrived, I had photos and materials to decorate the books flung all over the room in a colorful array. She laughed.

"No wonder you called me," she said. "This is chaos."

Shortly after we started work, the doorbell rang and I heard the door open. In a few moments Alba appeared in the bedroom.

"What a mess," she said.

Then she realized that we were looking at pictures of the past.

"I would like to see photos of Lily and Ellie," she said.

We brought out their childhood photos. They were lovely in their ruffles and bows. Both sisters were beauties. Lily's beauty was more pronounced. Ellie had a soft, lovely face. Her large eyes stared gently from the page.

"She was very beautiful," Alba said.

"Yes," I said, "both of them were exceptional women. One picture revealed Lily with the gold chain and the Alabama Crystal around her neck. Alba stared at it a long time and then at Kat's neck, where it now hung.

"Are you going to use the crystal," Alba asked.

"I already have," Kat said. Then she explained about her business and the success that she felt would continue.

"What happens to it now," Alba asked.

"I'm not sure," Kat said. "I'm still thinking about that myself."

Alba stayed with us a long time, looking at the pictures, and offering to help paste them into the scrapbooks. Then she said that she had to go into town. We were sorry to see her go. She was a fast, efficient worker. Kat and I finally finished our project. We had eight albums each, but they were finally under control. We threw away all the old boxes they had been stashed in. Kat and I had coffee and talked about the party. The phone rang; it was Mrs. Crank.

She asked if I was busy and I said, "No, just having coffee with Kat." She asked if I would visit her and bring Kat with me. We were both excited as we drove down. Hopefully Mrs. Crank had secured even more social events for Kat, and wanted to tell us in person. Mrs. Crank seemed happy to see us there. Kat complimented her on her window dressing and canopy. She was pleased. We were sitting on the covered porch at the home when a woman walked out to join us. It took a minute to recognize that the woman was Alba. Her hair was down and loose around her shoulders. It was a shiny grey with a minimum of tiny brown strands, a reminder of former youth.

She wore a white shirt and slacks. Tiny gold earrings decorated her ears in an appealing way.

"Alba," Kat said, "you look great."

Alba smiled and thanked her.

"I love the new you," I said.

"Good," she replied. "I hope you continue to do so."

She looked at Mrs. Crank, who was busy taking some papers from inside her jacket. Mrs. Crank smiled at her and turned my way.

"I have some things that I need to say to all of you," she said "Things that Alba already knows. You two have been kept in the dark way too long.

"Let me tell you my story. I grew up in Wayward with your Aunt El and Lily. Ellie was my best friend. I went away to college, then I married and moved here. After the fire that destroyed Ellie's house, I returned to see if she might need my assistance. She said that she had received enough money from the sale of the land to survive very well. Then she asked a favor of me.

"She had mourned the loss of her child for many years. She asked me to try to find Reuben Birdsong and her child. I told her that I would do so. For years after Ellie's death I searched for the missing child. None of the private detectives I hired were able to help me. Finally I hired a Native American named Firecross. Within a few weeks he brought me evidence that he had located Reuben Birdsong. He said Reuben was deceased and that he was survived by one child, a female. He persisted until he located the child and then contacted me.

"It turns out that Alba is the daughter that was taken from Ellie. I found this out last year and shared the news with her. She had a difficult time accepting it. It was quite a coincidence that the two of you had been neighbors and friends for years. Reuben Birdsong led his daughter to believe that her mother was dead. She was raised on the reservation and assisted the shaman there in the study of herbs and roots. Later, Alba decided to leave the reservation. Obviously, the fates led her to the house she purchased beside of you.

"For the past year I have been sharing old photographs of Ellie with her. I had one of Reuben and Ellie shortly after their marriage. I am sorry it has taken so long to tell you but I wanted to respect Alba's wishes. We have solid proof of the relationship.

"All I can say now is, girls, meet your cousin!"

We sat stunned, staring at Alba, uncertain of what to say. She seemed anxious also. Suddenly tears filled her eyes and she said, "This is my new look for my new life. I am so happy. I always mourned my dead mother. To be related to my two best friends is a miracle."

"No wonder you were so good with the bow and arrow," I said. That seemed to break the silence as everybody laughed.

"I can't believe it," Kat said. "We thought we had no family left."

"I thought the same thing," Alba said.

Mrs. Crank seemed very proud of herself.

Suddenly, Kat spoke up, "The Alabama Crystal," she said. "I think this should be yours now." She took it from around her neck and fastened it onto Alba's.

"I know you know some of the history behind the crystal, but I can explain further, "Alba announced. "My grandfather told me that long ago there was a special crystal. He said that my mother's family owned it, but that his ancestors had owned it first. My father made a special point to meet and marry the woman who had the crystal. After my birth, he had to return to his family. He knew that the woman would not be accepted, so he took me and left to raise me in tribal custom. I think he missed my mother deeply, but he had a great loyalty to the tribe. My grandfather asked me not to reveal to my father that I knew the true story. I agreed, to spare my father any further grief. This crystal has made a circle. All of us here are part of the circle."

"But why did he leave the crystal behind," I asked.

"My grandfather was a shaman. He could foretell the future," Alba said. "I imagine as a seer, he knew that the crystal would return in its own time."

Mrs. Crank said she was ready to go inside. She seemed tired, but happy, that she had completed her promise to her best friend.

The three of us met back at my house. We called Katie, Mandy, and Darrie to come over for an emergency meeting of the round table. While we waited, we looked at the scrapbooks with renewed interest. We promised to share them with Alba. I desperately wished that Aunt El could be here. How much Alba would have loved her.

Chapter Forty-One

Reuben Birdsong stood outside of the tipis of his father and grandfather. For centuries the tipis had changed hands, and the sweat and blood of the ancestors had imprinted a sheen into the sleek poles. The long pine poles rose eighteen feet in length, their bones covered by buffalo hides. The painting on the outside was distinct and beautiful. It was unique to his family, and painted in the sacred secrecy of his tribe. Pressed into the once-pliant pine shelf of one pole was a pair of beautiful crystals, identical in appearance. Beside of them lay a turquoise stone, and a black rock.

Reuben was listening to the sun power of the river, rushing in dark blue water over the rocks. He could hear the song of healing that his father was singing from the river to use on the wounded and ill. It was an honor to be the son of a singer. Reuben was well loved and respected by his tribe. He was meant to follow in his father's footsteps if the elders of the sky bestowed the gift of singing. Reuben could see the fish flash in sudden leaps from the water. He loved the colors they reflected in the sun, but he did not fish. Like the other Blackfeet men, he believed they were unfit for consumption. His skill as a hunter was greatly admired, as he was capable of bringing down buffalo and elk at good distances. The cool, clear Montana air drifted across the water as his father sang. Soon it would be time for his long robe. He lifted his arms to the sun, and his deer-antler bracelets rattled as he gave his prayer of thankfulness for the day. His tribe believed that the sun was the source of all power. Finally the song of his father stopped, and Reuben approached him. His father was tall, his dark hair streaked now with gray. He stood quietly as Reuben approached.

"My son," he said, "I have sung for the spirits and our ancestors have answered."

Reuben sensed what his next words would be, but remained silent. His father said that the healing crystals must lie in threes and that the third must be recovered for the prosperity of the tribe. Reuben nodded. He had grown up on the stories of the three crystals. One had been stolen long ago, and the power of the crystals would not return to full strength until its return. His father turned to him and grasped his shoulders.

"You are a man now," he said, "and you must help me return the crystal to our tribe. I must send you on a journey."

His father prepared a potion that the spirits had indicated to him in singing. He told Reuben that the crystal was in a small town in Georgia. He explained the history of the crystal once more and where to find it. "There is a girl there your age. You must gain her love and trust so that she will return the crystal to you. The spirits have told me that the way to do this is through marriage. Once you have the crystal you must return here."

"What about the girl," Reuben asked. "If she is to be my wife, does this mean that she, too, may return by my side?"

"No, the return of the girl would create confusion for the crystals. She must remain with her people. Only the crystal and anything that belongs to you may return. Leave nothing behind that is yours."

Reuben left the next morning. He slipped quietly from the reservation and traveled far south. He found a job with a construction crew that was arriving in town at the same time that he was. He was tall like his father, muscular, and very strong. He searched for Ellie as his father had instructed, watching her at her home doing chores.

One evening just as he was finishing work and receiving his pay, Ellie walked by. He waited while she went into a store. The other men scattered for home, but Reuben held his position. He was nervous and inexperienced with females, but he was determined. He need not have worried. Ellie was fascinated by his good looks and courteous ways. He asked her to allow him to buy her a soda and she agreed. Her big eyes smiling up at him so trustingly instilled a sort of warmth in him that he had never experienced before. They agreed to meet again. Ellie secured the job as a secretary and continued to see Reuben. She loved him deeply and could listen for hours as he spoke of the beauty of the mountains and the spirits that sang. It was only natural that they made love. Ellie was even more beautiful in love. When she discovered she was pregnant, she felt a total love and trust that things would work out. After all, once she was married, the Alabama Crystal would be passed down to her from her mother. The wedding was beautiful and simple. Ellie felt that her life was complete and could barely stand the wait to hold her baby in her arms. She was sure that Reuben would make an excellent father. When she gave birth, she tried desperately to glimpse the baby as it was swooped away. The women handed the baby over to Reuben, and begin administering help to Ellie, who was bleeding a bit more than normal. The women worked hard.

Finally Ellie's pleading to hold her baby, and the fact that she seemed perfectly fine, sent one of them into the yard to look for Reuben. No one could understand where he had disappeared to. It was unusual conduct, but he was the father. Perhaps it was a spiritual ritual that his family favored with newborns. Ellie knew that he was from a reservation, but he had refused to speak of his past, and she was too happy with their present and future to pursue anything else. She believed that in his own time, he would reveal his childhood and past.

Throughout the day, Ellie waited with worry for her newborn, but with faith in her husband. By nightfall, her worry had been replaced by a horror too difficult to think of. Intermingled with the horror was a deep confusion. She loved Reuben. She knew that he loved her. Why would he take their child away? Where was he? It wasn't until the next morning that they realized he wasn't coming back. Everything he owned was missing from his and Ellie's bedroom. There was no trace of him left to follow.

Chapter Forty-Two

The woman handed the baby to him hurriedly, her attention drawn toward the young mother and the possibility of distress. Reuben stared into the dark eyes of his daughter and held her high. It was then that the gift of his heritage fell upon him and he sang to the sun and to the mountains, sent his soothing chant into the mother earth, so that she might bear witness to this child and send blessings. He flung his knapsack over his shoulder and his daughter lay in his arms as he made his way home. The Alabama Crystal had lain in his young wife's hands as she had prayed for a safe delivery. He could not understand what had come over him. When the child was delivered to him, when his blessing had been heard, the only crystal that Reuben could see lay in the wide innocent stare of his daughter's eyes staring into his. The light reflected tiny crystal sparks in the deep brown.

He took off walking and arrived in the next town, where he was given a ride by a traveling salesman. By the time he reached Montana, his heart lay in a quandary of confusion and longing. As his father had demanded, his young wife had been left behind, but for the first time Reuben realized that much of his spirit remained with her. He hoped that his father would sing the healing song to drive her gentle eyes from his head, where her soft smile and warm arms reached for him again and again. The baby was quiet and traveled well. Reuben stopped in fields and milked cows, filling a small leather pouch in which he'd made a tiny hole that she could nurse through. He was uneasy at the thought of his father's wrath surely awaiting him. When he finally arrived at the reservation, his father watched his approach in silence. Reuben could hardly bear to meet his eyes, but his father was regarding him kindly and with compassion.

"I see you have brought my grand-daughter," he said, reaching for the small bundle. He studied her for a moment and then looked to his son. "She has the eyes of a singer," he said. Reuben nodded. His father studied the child carefully. She was very beautiful, the only hint that her heritage was anything other than Blackfoot was the fair skin and delicate nose. These she had inherited from her mother. Reuben could barely wait for him to finish his inspection of the baby. Her name was still hidden until a ceremony could be performed. Finally his father nodded his great approval and returned the child to him. Reuben took her in his arms and asked, "May I return and bring the mother here?"

His father frowned. "Only the child may stay; the woman belongs with her family." Other elders in the tribe were gathering around them. To disrespect his father in public by protesting would bring shame on his father and on himself. He nodded in agreement to his father's wishes.

"I failed to return the crystal," Reuben said, his eyes lowered in the misery of failure.

"You have not failed," his father said. "This child will return the crystal to our people. We have cleared the path for the return; she will walk the path."

Reuben was uncertain of his father's meanings, but he said nothing. He was tired from the journey and longing for the tipi and the buffalo blankets. As if reading his mind, his father gestured and a young squaw led him to his bed.

In the early morning, after he had rested, the young woman returned, her blanket with her. Nude, she slipped beneath the covers and became the woman of Reuben. The young squaw was widowed and childless. Her husband had lost his life from a snake bite, and her loneliness was alive in her eager eyes. She took over the care of the baby. At the naming ceremony, the true name was whispered and the spoken name was announced. The spoken name of Reuben's daughter was Alba. As soon as Alba could run, she ran to her grandfather, and spent hours just listening and watching as he told stories of their people. Reuben loved to teach her the traditions, and the songs of the tribe. She was a quick learner, far faster than he had been. Alba knew that the young squaw was not her mother. When she questioned her father he told her that her mother had died while giving her life. She absorbed this unchangeable fact with sadness and acceptance. Reuben loved Alba deeply, and ignored tradition by having her schooled outside of the reservation. When she completed high school, he sent her to college.

Often he longed to tell her the truth of her birth. Most of all, he longed to see Ellie, for it was a terrible discovery to find that he could not forget her. Her love for him and faith in him was like a hot iron across his heart. He remembered her trust and the way she had leaned upon him with confidence throughout the pregnancy.

Torn between his heritage and his heart, he often wondered if he had made the right choice. At first he had not returned because of his loyalty to the tribe and to his father. Later, it was the terrible shame at the pain he had created in an innocent life that kept him from taking Alba and returning to the only woman he was ever destined to love.

When Alba returned from college, she began teaching the children of the tribe and provided an education for them that they would never have achieved without her knowledge from the outside world. She also practiced healing and the different properties of the plants, bark, and bushes around her. Plants seemed to sprout magically full and healthy beneath her touch. At last Reuben decided to approach her with the true story of her mother. He realized that his decision so long ago had created emptiness, not only in his life, but also in the life of his daughter. He was saddened for the young wife and mother who had never held her baby in her arms. He knew in his heart that she had spent her life nurturing others, and giving to other children what she could never give to her own child. He sang to the spirits and told his intentions in the song of request. If answered correctly, he would the approval of the spirits to reveal the true facts of her birth to Alba.

***

Reuben sat one night watching the fire. The sun had gone down but he could feel the power of the silver stars and the rush of wind that came down from the mountain pass. For many months he had felt the change of his heartbeat and a tiredness that seemed to weary his bones. Alba was on a call to the tipis of the village to work with the children that needed more individual attention. After a petition to the gods, he lay down to rest. Sometime in the middle of the night, Reuben heard the singing of his dead father. He felt a great lightness of body. His spirit yearned toward the voice.

As he lay quietly in his tipi, his spirit broke free to roam the wild hills with his father. When Alba returned she lay across the body of her father in grief. She begin to wail a song of transport for his soul. She grieved for the great heart that had broken into the next world, where she could not touch him again until her own death. She notified the elders and they came for his body.

Three weeks after the death of her father, Alba left the reservation for good. She heard a soft whisper of her name in the spring breezes. She traveled from town to town for many years, always returning for brief visits to the reservation. She had resolved herself to traveling. For several years she travels the back roads and felt the freedom of the wind behind her back. Finally, she arrived in Ashford, Virginia. She was older now and tired. She decided to put down roots.

Chapter Forty-Three

The girls arrived looking worried. It was very, very rare for an emergency meeting to be called. We sat down and told them the entire story. They were wide-eyed. Katie squealed excitedly and grabbed Alba.

"This is too much to believe", she said, "but it is so wonderful. It boggles the mind. I imagine this is the work of the Alabama Crystal!"

Mandy and Darrie had a dozen questions for us to answer. Everything had changed so suddenly. It was strange to have a cousin, but also exciting. All of those years as neighbors had acquainted us very well. Alba was already our family before it became official. With the secret out, Alba seemed younger and happier. Her new look updated her to the present times.

"I wish I had known my mother," Alba said. "To think of all the years we could have been together. She was very beautiful. I love the photos."

"I would find it hard to forgive him if he were my father," Katie said.

"No," she said slowly, "he was a victim of his heritage. He was a wonderful father. I think he loved my mother. I know that he never remarried. Tribes are terribly enmeshed and loyalty is a major part of our customs."

"No wonder you and Kat are so competitive with cooking," Katie said. "Great cooks obviously run in the family."

"That is true enough," Alba said, "and let me say that I have more experience."

"Really," Kat said. "Well, I have more recipes!"

Now the two of them could compete in a friendly way, knowing that cooking was in both of their genes.

"You know, there are still two things that you do not know about me," Alba said.

"What?" Kat and I asked in the same breath.

"Well, I love to sing. I have it in my blood, so the competition that you receive at the next karaoke may be daunting to your high levels of confidence." We laughed.

"Good," Kat said, "then maybe we could convince you to join us at Sing and Serve."

"No, thank you," Alba said, "but I might join you at the club the next time all of you go out. I will be a tough act to follow."

"Then we won't follow you," Katie said earnestly. "We shall wait for the monotone woman. The audience is always hysterical with relief when someone takes her place onstage." We all laughed and agreed that we should make plans to go out the following weekend.

"I suppose a love of singing was woven throughout the family. I know a few chants I might teach you, and you can teach me to sing country." She seemed to find the idea very amusing.

"Wait a second," Kat said, "you said two things. What's the other thing?"

"Well, the second thing is my name," Alba said.

"You mean your name isn't Alba," I said in surprise.

She laughed. "Oh no," she said. "That's my nickname. My full name is Alabama Crystal Birdsong."

About the Author

Phibby Venable is an Appalachian poet and writer. Her work appears in numerous anthologies, magazines, ezines, and journals, both nationally and internationally, including:

Clinch Mountain Review, 2River, Poetrybay, Southern Ocean Review, the Appalachian Review, the Sow's Ear Review, and the Circle Magazine.

She has three chapbooks: What I Saw Beautiful, Indian Wind Song, and On White Top.

Two full collections include Blue Cold Morning, and Blue Water Poems.

Phibby is active in both human and animal rescue.